AMBUSHED!

"Brother John, there's a story about this camp that you're that ornery, no-account, killing, robbing Comanche John, and I want ye to know I'm taking no belief in it."

"Thank-ee," said John. "Only I hear he ain't so bad. Steals from the rich to give to the poor. Confines his killin' strictly to varmints, Abolitionists, and that ilk."

He ate, wiped up the last bit of gravy on a biscuit, ate that, and dropped the plate back in the plunder box. Then he cut over through the river brush to the spot where he'd left his bed.

Suddenly he was aware of danger—a slight movement, a sound, a danger he seemed to *smell*. What caused him to dip his head and dive forward he never knew, but he *did*—and powder flame burst in his face, and there was a wind whip of lead passing, plucking at the crown of his black slouch hat. . . .

Other *Leisure* books by Dan Cushman:

THE ADVENTURES OF COMANCHE JOHN
BLOOD ON THE SADDLE
NO GOLD ON BOOTHILL
THE PECOS KID
THE PECOS KID RETURNS
THE SILVER MOUNTAIN

THE RETURN OF COMANCHE JOHN

DAN CUSHMAN

LEISURE BOOKS NEW YORK CITY

A LEISURE BOOK ®

September 2004

Published by special arrangement with Golden West Literary Agency.

Dorchester Publishing Co., Inc.
200 Madison Avenue
New York, NY 10016

ISBN 0-8439-5388-8

Visit us on the web at www.dorchesterpub.com.

Table of Contents

Land of the I-de-ho

I

"A WEARY PILGRIM"

There was a bite of winter in the air, making the black-whiskered man shiver and draw his buckskin jacket more snugly around his shoulders. He pulled his slouch hat down, too, and he scrunched a trifle over the neck of his gunpowder roan pony, all without taking his eyes off the mountain valley below. It lay lifeless, not even a deer browsing, the spruce timber green-purple-black, the brush tinted ruddy from frost, and the river, the Lemhi, like a winding strip of metal.

After he had been there a considerable time, a rider appeared, cantering warily as befitted a white man in that year of 1863, rifle across the pommel of his saddle. He rode on for half a mile until he had a long view of the valley ahead, then he climbed his horse to a small promontory and signaled with high sweeps of his hat. Soon afterward the black-whiskered man heard the distant shouts and rattles of a wagon train. He grunted his satisfaction and spat a long stream of tobacco juice.

"Why, thar they be," he said. "Damned if they didn't make it nigh on schedule."

He took time now to scratch all through his black whiskers. His age could have been anywhere from thirty-five to forty-five. His skin was browned the hue of saddle leather.

He was shorter than average and somewhat broader, a breadth accentuated by his long-stirruped manner of sitting a horse. His hat was a black slouch sombrero, his jacket was squaw-made with here and there some beadwork, his trousers were gray homespun. He wore jackboots pulled up to protect his knees from the brush that grew thickly in these Idaho mountains. Around his waist on crossed belts was a brace of Colts, Navy model, cap-and-ball, caliber .36.

He was in no hurry. He watched the wagon train come lurching into sight, one and two outfits at a time, and roll into a circle. The first wagoners immediately started a fire, but stragglers kept coming in for half an hour, and now early darkness was settling.

The whiskered man counted nine covered wagons and seventeen supply wagons, most of the latter hitched two in tandem, and there were a couple of carts. The draft stock was all horse and mule, which was a fool chance to take with Bannocks and Palouses on the prowl now that that blasted Abe Lincoln had pulled all the federal troops home trying to lick the Confederacy. Oxen, that's what emigrants should drive, because no Indian would bother much to get an ox. The cattle, mongrel-looking milk stock, were being herded by a kid on horseback.

They were camped now and all seemed safe enough. No vigilante sign. He nudged the gunpowder pony and rode down, still watchful, still wary. On the breeze came an odor of cooking that made his stomach go bottomless from hunger and over the talk, and the *whack* of axes, and the *clatter* of pans, came a voice and a banjo. It was a very clear and flexible tenor voice, and the words made the black-whiskered man sit up, and open his eyes with delight, for he was Comanche John, and the song was about him.

Oh, gather 'round ye teamster men
And listen to my tale
Of the worst side-windin' varmint
That rides the outlaw trail.
He wears the name Comanche John
And he comes from old Missou',
Where many a Concord coach he stopped
And many a gun he drew.

Then a man bellowed in a rough, nasal voice: "Rusty, stop singing about that road agent varmint or, by grab, you'll get fed hide, horns, and taller for supper!"

The banjo stopped, and another man said: "Aw, let him sing, Lafe. I think I'd've gone crazy already if it hadn't been for his singin' and banjoin'."

"Well, let him sing and banjo something besides that road agent doggerel. He ain't sung another thing since he heerd it offen the freighters the other side of Fort Hall."

"A very beautiful piece," said Comanche John, riding into the firelight. "Have ye ever heered the verse that goes?:

Comanche rode to Yallerjack
In the year of 'Sixty-Two,
With Three-Gun Bob and Dillon
And a man named Henry Drew.
They robbed the stage, they robbed the bank,
They robbed the Western mail,
And many a cheek did blanch to hear
Their names spoke on the trail."

"I never heard that one!" cried a good-natured-looking man, short and powerful, with hair and whiskers in a tangle, grayish from wagon dust. "Ahoy, stranger, you look like

13

you'd traveled a piece. You come from the upper Yallerstone? You come from the gold fields?"

The black-whiskered man sat his horse between two of the wagons, at the edge of the firelight. "I come from a heap o' places far and near, a weary pilgrim." He sniffed the odor of biscuits baked in Dutch ovens buried in the flames. "Share and share alike, that's my motto."

"Well, you're welcome to 'light."

Men were coming as the word traveled swiftly that a stranger from the gold fields of Montana country was in camp. He watched them, slouched to one side, a posture that brought the butt of his right-hand Navy Colt away from his hip; he chawed sleepily; he yawned, but his eyes were ever narrow and alert.

He called: "Be they one amongst ye by the handle of the Reverend Jeremiah Parker?"

A big, red-whiskered man bellowed—"The parson?"— and came up with a heavy-footed, tired man's limp. "Say, are you the guide that was to meet us at Fort Hall?"

"Now, I might be, but I didn't promise to meet ye at Fort Hall. The parson said Fort Hall or the Lemhi, and this be the Lemhi."

"Well," the big man said, rubbing his chin, "you're welcome to 'light and have grub, but I guess we got over needing a guide."

Comanche John said mildly: "I rode five, six sleeps across some mighty rough country to meet this train and guide it to the Bitterroot, and, whilst I'm in favor of an outfit being able to change its mind, on t'other hand I don't like it to be quite that free with my time." He spat, and added: "And my horse don't, neither."

Lafe said to the red-whiskered one: "Listen, Stocker, that was never put to a vote."

Stocker, rearing his shoulders up in a bull-moose posture, shouted: "Dammit, no matter what he says, he was to meet us at Fort Hall! He's late and we don't need him!"

"Well . . . let's take it up later with Wood."

"We don't *need* to take it up with Wood."

Comanche John dismounted painfully. He limped around getting the stiffness out of his joints. "I ain't the man I used to be," he muttered, "I ain't for a fact. I'm going to find me a squaw and settle down."

They had sent for the Reverend Jeremiah Parker. He came at a half lope, a spare old man with wispy gray hair that fell over his shoulders, a shaved face, and a neck like a plucked rooster's. Behind him was a kid of fifteen trying to get him to put on a black greatcoat.

"John!" cried the Reverend Parker, stopping and stretching his arms half toward the black-whiskered man and half toward the heavens. "*John!* I told 'em you'd come. I prayed, too. And all the while I could feel the power of those prayers like a rope dragging you across those mountains."

"If ye don't mind," said John, "I'd just as lief you didn't mention that word *rope* in my presence."

The parson came closer, staring at him with his protruding, Old Testament eyes. "John, you ain't tooken to your old ways!"

"I'm innocent as a babe unborn, and mighty nigh as bankrupt. I given up the ways of sin and its wages, too. May I be struck with lightning if I had my hand in a single robbery except for maybe one coach, and that because it had Union money in it, and no sin for me, Parson, because it was an act of war, me being a Confederate!"

"Well . . . ," said the parson, and decided to let it pass. "What name you going by?"

"Smith. Sometimes I call myself Jones, and sometimes

15

Brown, but generally just plain Smith. It's not so unusual . . . attracts less attention."

"Hush!" said the parson. "Here comes trouble."

A very handsome, well-built man of about thirty was just walking up in the strong light of the fire. He was not an ordinary wagoner. There was something of the aristocrat in his bearing. He was dressed in antelope-skin breeches and shirt and a very wide beaver hat. The garb was ordinary enough on the frontier, but his air and body gave it quality. Around his waist, buckled high, was a new Army .44 and a patent powder ball-and-cap dispenser. His eyes were on John. He nodded. There was a cold courtesy in his smile.

"This be John Smith," said the parson.

"Royal," the man said, and the name fit him. "I'm Dave Royal. I'm guiding the wagon train. I'm sorry if there was some misunderstanding."

"I doubt there's been one."

The smile left Royal's lips, but he came on to shake John's hand anyway. "You were to meet us at Fort Hall," he said. "You weren't there."

As if to drive this home, Royal came down hard on John's hand, showing his strength—and he was very strong. Caught unaware, it seemed to John that the bones in his hand were being ground to splinters, but he took the pain with no change of expression.

"You're a mighty strong man, Mister Royal. Mightee strong. And now if ye will let me have my hand back. . . ."

"*Right* then about Fort Hall? *Right?*" Showing his teeth, he came down a trifle harder when he said *"Right"* and a trifle harder still when he said it again.

Comanche John had shifted his weight slightly. He thrust his left shoulder low and forward. He turned, stepped with his left foot behind Royal's right knee, and placed his foot on the man's left toe.

Royal had a flash of what he intended and tried to drop the hand and step clear, but he was tripped up. He found himself suddenly propelled forward. His feet were off the ground, his abdomen borne by the fulcrum of John's left shoulder, and he was deposited in a sprawled position, on his back, on the ground.

He lay for half a second in shock. His hat rolled off. His hair was knocked over his eyes. He recovered and twisted over then, with a quickness surprising for one of his size, and his right hand went for the .44 Army Colt, but Comanche John, with a casual, hitching movement, had already unholstered his left-hand Navy, and had it aimed.

Royal froze. His mouth was slightly open. He did not breathe. The gun muzzle held him hypnotized. It was so quiet for the space of three or four seconds that one could hear the snap of logs in the big cook fire.

"Now that trick," said John, "I learnt offen the Comanches, whose specialty is wrestling. And if ye ever try to stronghand me again, I'll show you a trick I learnt from Wild Bill Graves, whose specialty was shooting men right betwixt the eyes."

Royal took his hand away from his gun. Still staring at the Navy, making every move slowly, like one who had awakened with a rattlesnake coiled by his bed and feared to startle it, he got his hands behind him and climbed to his feet.

"Thar," said John. "That's the ticket. 'The meek shall inherit the earth.' I'm a man of religious leanings myself. Yea, I am a stranger amongst ye with my back turned on the black gulch of sin, and that's straight from the psalms of David . . . it is for a fact." He holstered his Navy.

Royal had recovered his composure and his fury. He was hollow-eyed and hollow-cheeked from fury. The muscles stood out at the sides of his jaw and the veins on his forehead. He had a hard time getting words to come through his taut lips: "Get out! Get out of this camp!"

John chawed, and spat, and moved back just a trifle farther into the shadows. He was wary of anyone behind him. He waited.

Royal looked around at the stunned wagoners, roughly dressed men, farming men, men uprooted by war and poverty, and he waited for them to do his bidding.

"Tell him to get out! Are you going to let him walk into this camp and threaten to kill? Tell him to go or by the gods. . . ."

"If you ask me, you had it coming!"

It was the raw voice of a woman. She was a gangling, tall woman, her height accentuated by a high-waisted calico dress that dragged and caught in grass and twigs as she walked. On her head was a long poke bonnet. Strapped around her waist was a double-barreled shot pistol, once a flintlock and now converted to percussion, a massive blunderbuss that weighed at least five pounds.

She stopped. She looked at Royal, and at the red-whiskered man, and all around at the wagoners, and she gave an especially long look at four rough-appearing, armed men who had come running over from their somewhat removed camp at the sound of trouble.

"Yes, you had it coming, Royal! Ever and a day showing off how strong you are, making like to bust the bones in a man's hand. You did it to Rusty once, fixed him so he couldn't play his poor little banjo for two days, but finally you run into your match!" Then she turned her attention to John. "Praise be to glory, did I hear you ejaculate that you were a religious man?"

"I hit the sawdust trail," said John piously, with his

18

thumbs hooked in his gun belts. "I turned my back on Rocky Bar, which is worse'n Sodom, and on Bannack City, which is nigh as bad as Gomorrah. I'm a pilgrim on the rocky trail o' life. I been buffeted by fate, and chased by the minions of the unrighteous."

"Glory amen!" she cried, lifting her arms in thanksgiving.

A trifle sourly, the red-whiskered Stocker said: "I hate to bring this up, Betsy, but he *does* seem to be a trifle weighted down with Sam Colt metal for a sky pilot."

"And why wouldn't he be, the company he has to keep? Tell me this, stranger, do ye believe in baptism by total immersion, or are you just a hair dipper?"

"I be a Methodist till I die!"

"Well," said Betsy with a slight diminution of enthusiasm, "I guess that'll have to do."

A small, middle-aged man had that moment ridden up and dismounted, and the crowd opened for him. He walked up thin and beat-out from the trail, but still carrying himself with vigor.

Betsy said: "Thar's Wood! Now we got somebody with *sense*."

"What's the excitement?" Wood asked.

It was evident that this man rather than Royal was their leader. Betsy started to answer, but he shook his head and indicated that he wanted to hear from Stocker.

"Why, this is the parson's guide. Just showed up. Rode in out of the night. Two weeks late."

"He made no agreement to meet us in Fort Hall, if that's what you mean," Wood said in a tired voice. "I've tried to tell you that. The parson asked him to meet us there, otherwise here on the Lemhi. Well, here he is. This is the Lemhi."

Stocker, scratching around at his tangled red hair, muttered: "Damn it, I say he should o' been at Fort Hall. Gettin'

19

his money damn' easy, showing here instead of Fort Hall."

Royal cried: "Send him on his way. I'm guiding the train. I have an agreement!"

Wood said: "Don't talk to me that way. I've told you before I'm not going to take any bullyragging."

A girl, a very pretty, dark-haired girl of seventeen or eighteen, had followed Wood into the light. A similarity in their manners revealed them to be father and daughter.

"Dave!" she said, staring at Royal in surprise. "What's the matter with you?"

"Sorry." He got control of himself. There were fragments of grass and twigs on his beaver hat and on his soft-rubbed antelope-skin shirt. He brushed himself off and fingered his wavy hair back into place. "I was just surprised to see your dad take the attitude he did. You know very well the agreement we had when I turned north with you at Bridger."

The parson started in on him, magpie-voiced, long-armed, and wild-haired, only to be checked by Wood.

"Never mind, Parson. Save it for Sunday. Right now we're all tired and hungry. We'll have a full meeting on it after supper. Anger never settled anything. And anger isn't going to settle anything, not here, not while I'm captain. Not ever!"

II

"RENEGADES IN THE TRAIN"

Comanche John, with his back propped against a wagon tongue, ate venison and dumplings, using his Bowie knife, and big Betsy Cobb kept filling his plate until he was forced to protest.

"Enough. By grab, enough! Woman, you'll spile me for heaven giving me food like that." Then he asked her: "Do you reckon Royal is aiming to fetch me some trouble guiding this wagon train over the Bitterroots?"

"I'll lay him low with a doubletree," muttered big Betsy from inside her wagon. "By the way, Brother John, be you a married man?"

"No-o," said John."

"I buried my husband." Betsy blew her nose. "On the Platte, t'other side of Fort Laramie. Died of the horse croup. It was a great shock to me. A dreadful shock." Then she brightened. "But the reverend preached a beautiful sermon. All about the land where we ne'er say good bye. A wonderful man, my Mister Cobb, though he *did* take a little drop of likker now and again." She looked down at him. "Brother John, I *do* hope you're not a drinking man."

Her unusual interest made John uncomfortable, so he got up to talk with the parson.

"Danged widda woman! Got her cap perched for me. By grab, I'm going to be hard to catch. When I settle down, it's a Blackfeet gal for me."

"Don't find squaws turning out her brand of stew," said the parson.

"True, but ye don't find a squaw that takes such a whopping big delight out o' burying her husband, either." He got his cheek loaded with blackjack natural twist and stood looking at the group of men gathered near Dave Royal. "*They* ain't farmers."

"Injun fighters, stringing along for the lift."

John recognized the type: frontier renegades, too lazy for work and not nervy enough for banditry.

"Who be the long, tall, limber one with the chawed-off whiskers?"

"Calls himself Vogel."

John remembered then. Ed Vogel, Placerville. He had shot a man in the back there. A gambler named Sagrue. Sagrue had just stepped down from the platform by the High Riffle, and there was Vogel with the Navy in the shadows. They'd have hanged him that night, but he took to the timber until the affair blew over. Later on, John had heard, he joined the Bobtail Spruce gang, and then turned them over to the vigilantes for a measly eighteen ounces of gold. All that had been years ago, back toward 1849, and he rather thought Vogel would be dead by this time, but he wasn't. He was alive, dirty and lousy as ever.

"Who's the others?"

"Short one's Little Tom. He's not so bad. Laughs and jokes all the time, but I'd guess he was on the run from *something*. Black one's Sanchez . . . he's Mex' . . . then the big fellow with the ox-yoke mustache is Moose Petley, used to be a whiskey trader among the Paiutes. And that sort of fat one is

Belly River Bob . . . he's drunk all the time."

"They're cooking up something for me, Parson, and I don't like it."

"Forget 'em. Joe Wood will keep these pilgrims in line. They complain, but they stick by him just the same. He swung this deal, you know. Bought the White Pine land from the old Western Fur Company at bankruptcy court in Saint Louis, bought 'er for a song, the finest land in all the Nor'west. Uncommonly smart man, Joe Wood. They'll meet, and they'll jaw, but they'll do what he says. And just between us, he's a mite suspicious of that Royal."

"How about his daughter?"

"Lela? Poor little dove! I tell you, John, it makes me choke up from sorrow thinking about her, trying to choose between Royal and that no-account banjo player, Rusty McCabe. She's seventeen, you know, and nigh onto being an old maid."

With supper finished, Joe Wood called the meeting as he had promised, and, although Ambrose Stocker had his say and a chinless, tall man named Wally Snite arose in opposition to taking on John as guide, there was no serious threat to Wood's leadership. In conclusion Wood said: "I don't expect any division of opinion about the route to the Bitterroot, anyhow. Royal will have his say. We all will have our say. And if there's any doubt, we'll vote on it."

That apparently satisfied everyone with the exception of Snite, who said nothing, and Royal, who shrugged and laughed it off. Later John saw Royal by the let-down steps of Wood's Conestoga wagon, talking to Lela, who sat with her knees drawn together, her arms wrapped around them, leaning forward, listening very intently.

"Varmint," he muttered. But you couldn't exactly blame

her. He was the handsome one!

He ambled on among the wagons toward a little cutbank among the spruce where Moose Petley, Sanchez, and Belly River Bob had built a fire and stretched some canvas against the wind that blew down coldly from the mountain passes. No sign of Vogel.

Moose Petley and Belly River Bob were engaged in an argument, their voices raised, cursing each other. Their argument concerned the shape of the world, with Petley maintaining it was round and Bob that it was flat.

John said, walking into the light of the wind-whipped fire: "You're both wrong. If ye want to know what the world is, it's square."

"Well, that's the damnedest fool thing I ever *did* hear," said Moose Petley, giving him an ugly stare and looking to be sure where his Navy was.

John said: "In the Old Testament it says so. Thar it is in black and white. 'They come from the four corners of the world.' And who be you, or me, or any of us, to argue with scripture?"

Moose shouted: "I don't care if the scripture says it or if the gov'ment says it, the world's round! There was a fellow sailed around it."

"Who was he?" asked Belly River Bob.

"I forget his name. He's dead now," answered Petley.

"You're damned right he's dead," put in John, "because if he sailed out there too far, he'd fall over the edge and that'd pretty well be the end of *him*."

"Well," Petley said, "how about those fellows, Chinee traders, sail from San Francisco to Canton, and around Good Hope to London, and then over to Noo Yawk, and maybe around the Horn to Californy again? How do you figure that?"

Bob said, spitting and wiping his chin: "I got that figured out, too. Only one answer to it. The world *is* round in a way, but not round like a ball, but round like a saucer. It *has* to be as anybody with common sense could see, because otherwise the oceans would all run out over the edge and it'd be dry land, dry as a bone. So these fellows that sail to Chinee just go out and get turned around somewhere."

They argued some more without Belly River Bob's giving an inch in his contention until Petley in a rage drew his Bowie and lunged forward with its needle-sharp point against Bob's stomach.

"Shut up, damn you!" he bellowed. "Shut up or I'll whack your liver out. If they's one thing I cain't stand, it's an ignorant man."

And Bob, believing him, fell silent.

"Well, stranger," Moose Petley said to John, sitting back cross-legged to pare his nails with the Bowie, "it ain't every day you find a man quitting the gold fields to guide an ornery wagon train like this, but I guess everybody to his own tastes."

"I've seen you some place," Bob said, "but I can't recollect."

"I been here and I been yonder," John said. "And as for me guiding this ornery wagon train, I'll just return the amazement, because it seems a bit strange you boys would pass up the gold camp turn-off yourselves. Don't tell me you're farmers. You ain't the type. I hazard a guess that the things you boys have planted along the way won't sprout till Judgment Day."

"Say, that's pretty good!" said Belly River Bob, slapping a filthy pants leg.

The Mexican, Sanchez, a very stocky man with a clean-shaved, oily-looking face now spoke: "*Señor*, you are very sharp at guessing professions. Could you guess mine? I am a barber. If you at any time decide you need a shave. . . ."

"You ain't going to get near *my* throat with no razor."

"Mine, neither," muttered Belly River Bob.

John had been stalling, watching for Vogel, and now he saw him, a long-armed, long-legged, double-jointed man, cutting over from Snite's wagon. He was dressed in homespuns, on his head was a hat so wide and floppy he had to fasten the brim to the crown to keep it from falling across his face, and on his feet were moccasins with the toes turned in after the manner of an Indian's. He carried two guns with the holsters fastened to his legs, their ends forward as the gun butts stuck back, threatening with each step to fall to the ground, but they never did.

"Well, good night to ye," said John to those at the fire, and sauntered over, meeting Vogel by apparent accident. "Hello, Vogel."

Vogel drew up. His eyes were shifty; his body became tense. "You know me?"

"Yes, and you know me, I reckon."

Vogel laughed then, showing a lot of tobacco-browned teeth that looked black in the half dark. "So that's it, you were afeared I'd talk."

"Not afeared. Just wanted to tell ye that if one of these mornings somebody calls me 'Comanche John', I'd walk right over and shoot you on general principles."

"You don't need to worry about me." Vogel was tensely serious, staring John in the eyes. "I'll not turn informer on my own kind."

"How about the Bobtail Spruce gang?"

"That's a dirty lie. When the Californy stranglers wasn't clever enough to get their ropes on me, they spread that story hoping one of the gang would kill me, but it's a lie."

26

Only John knew it was not a lie. He bade Vogel good night, and went over for his bedroll.

"You're welcome to pitch camp in my wagon," said the parson, but John refused, saying he was "a creetur of the free and open," and carried his robes down toward the river.

He knew that a man was following, so he waited. The man was Dave Royal.

"Here I be," said John.

Royal had long ago recovered from his anger. He walked up, and with perfect, although slightly cold, civility, he asked: "How much have they offered you to guide them to White Pine?"

"Maybe not a cent."

Royal let a laugh jerk his shoulders. "What could be your purpose?"

John thought of saying—*What could be yours?*—but he decided to go easy and not start a ruckus. He said: "That ornery old parson . . . he saved my hide one time. My *neck,* I should say. Accused of highway robbery. Of course, I was innocent as a babe unborn. But he saved me. Saved my neck and then he took enough interest in me to save my eternal soul from the fires of hell. Oh-h! what a hell that parson did save me from! A fearful place. One night in his sermon he had 'em stretched out on those Cherokee drying frames with hot coals all over their bare backs, and thar was screaming and gnashing of teeth, and the parson told how the hair and flesh smelled burning that way . . . well, 'twas enough to give a person the fan-tods. Make him examine his conscience. How long has it been since you examined your conscience, Royal?"

"My conscience serves me." He had taken some currency from a belt inside his antelope shirt. "There's two hundred dollars here," he said. "Enough to buy you stage passage from Bannack Pass to Salt Lake. I think you'd winter much better in Salt Lake than in the deep snow at White Pine."

"What's them . . . greenbacks? Wuthless Union paper. Likely Robbie Lee has tooken Washington by this time. Getting mighty close, last dispatch I seen. That scroll ain't worth more'n ten cents on the dollar."

"Would you take gold?"

He looked at him, narrow-eyed. "You'd pay *gold* to git rid o' me? Why?"

Royal showed traces of a brittle temper once again. "What do you care as long as you're paid?"

John, leaning against a tree, scratched his back, and chawed, and kept his thumbs hooked in his twin gun belts. His right hand was still slightly lame from the breaking Royal had tried to give it.

"Well?" said Royal.

"Waal, no."

Royal, with a little tight tremble appearing in his voice, said: "Don't let me see you around here after breakfast tomorrow!" Turning on his heel he walked off.

John called after him: "And if ye do?" But Royal did not answer him.

III

"GUNFIGHT LESSON"

With days growing short and a feel of blizzard in the air, the wagon train did not wait for dawn. A bell clanged out, awakening the camp while it was still dark, with stars out and the night frost still stiffening the grass. The stock was brought in; amid the shouts and curses of men, the wagons were hitched. The first wagons started out, gee-hawing and creaking through the cold, while the more tardy ones were still unhitched.

There was no communal fire this morning; from several wagon stovepipes smoke was coming and the occupants of these had warm breakfasts, but others ate cold dummy as they walked beside their teams, swinging their whips, fighting to get away first, to win a margin of distance against possible delay from breakdown, to get first chance at the grass. Making it over the pass or being left stranded along the way would depend on a man's stock, and a horse or mule pulled his weight or fell in the traces depending on the food he found along the way.

John found big Betsy Cobb working like a man, backing a team of refractory bays up to the trees. She brushed off his offer to help. There was no chance for hot breakfast there, so

John walked on to help the parson, who drove an old Conestoga held together by rawhide pulled by a wiry four-horse team of Indian ponies.

"By grab," said John, "I wouldn't drive this outfit a mile for water. I'd pack-saddle over the hump and leave this wagon behind."

"She rattles," said the parson, "but she's tough. Don't let that rawhide fool you. Now you take two pieces of oak doweled and mortised together, give it a bend, and what happens? . . . she breaks, especially in the dry climate. But rawhide *gives*. New wagon is too stiff. Give me an old one every time. This 'un crawls over the rocks like a snake."

John said casually: "Royal tried to hire me to git out last night."

"He *did?* Well, I'm going to see Wood about. . . ."

"Keep it to yourself, Parson. I won't rest easy until I learn what that rangy wolf is after."

John scouted ahead on a borrowed horse, giving the gunpowder a chance to graze. From a high pinnacle he saw the wagon train strung out along miles of valley. He rested, napped, and still he could see it, moving so slowly.

To the east and north rose the Bitterroots, already white with snow. In the west were the low, rounded summits of the Salmon River Range, all misty autumn purple. In another day they would reach Salmon River and follow it briefly until it made its big swing to the west, when their trail would keep going north, up, up, and up to the ridge of the world, the main range of the Rockies, before dropping down on Bitterroot River.

As yet, Royal had done nothing to back up the threat he had made. John had supper with the parson and warmed his boots at the fire, listening to the singing of young Rusty

McCabe. Later he carried his robes down to the river brush as he had the night before, but he was suspicious and stayed clear of his bed to wait and watch.

The big fire died; the camp grew silent; the moon rose. After half an hour, when John was almost ready to give it up, a man appeared, rising from the shadows no more than the length of a picket rope away. He had not seen or heard him come; he was just there, like the spirit his pappy had seen rising from the earth of a graveyard when he was a boy. Only that spirit Pappy saw was misty gray-white, and this one was black.

John could not be certain who it was. The man went poking carefully through the trees, and John waited, expecting the crash of a pistol shot when he found the bedroll, but the shot did not come, and at last he went back and found his bed untouched.

Still, for safety's sake he moved it, and next day, riding scout in advance of the wagon train, he was careful to keep clear of ambush. He had no hint of his night visitor, and he almost dismissed the matter from his mind.

The country had broadened out, with small hills almost devoid of timber. Next day the Lemhi joined the Salmon. There was grass aplenty here, grass that blew waves in the wind, grass belly-deep to the stock. He located Joe Wood's wagon and rode down, finding Lela in the high seat, handling the lines.

"Where's your pa?" he asked, and there was something peculiar in her manner when she pointed toward a couple of men on horseback half a mile away.

The men were Joe Wood and a young, very red-faced farmer named O'Donnell.

"If I was a farmer," John said, jogging the gunpowder into talking range, "damned if I wouldn't stop right here. I

31

been up and down this country for many a year, and this Salmon beats 'em all."

"We already own our land," Wood said with a tight set to his lips. "We'll go on to the White Pine."

"So I figured." He nodded toward the grass. "You won't find such feed when the mountains commence, and that'll be damned sudden. Mighty long haul to the top and mighty long on t'other side. I know there's blizzard in the air, but if this was my outfit, I'd camp maybe two days, gamble that way, just to put some strength in the horses." He could tell that something was troubling Wood, so he said: "Out with it! Whatever ye got in your craw."

"I've been told you're a bandit on the jump from the vigilantes over in the Montana."

John thought about it for a long time, squinting off while his jaw slowly revolved on his chew of tobacco. "Mighty big, this country. Might-ee broad, and twice as wild. This be the wild Nor'west, and she's different than Missouri. Ye meet a man out on the trail, and ye don't ask who he was, or what he was. It's what he *is* that counts. Which bandit am I supposed to be, Whiskey George, or Zip Skinner, one o' them?"

"Comanche John."

"Yip-ee!" said John. "Why, that's top riffle. Why, *I'm* the most famous road agent of 'em all. *I'm* the one they wrote the song about!"

O'Donnell in his serious manner said to Wood: "I would rather be trusting *him*."

"Never mind," said Wood.

They decided to lay over one day for the grass and to make wagon repairs before the tough climb began. All day John was aware of the talk being circulated against him, not only that he was Comanche John, but that he was in league with the remnants of the Snake River Gang, that the Snake River Gang might well be waiting in ambush to get their horses and supplies once they were on the Bitterroot side. By the time darkness came, the suspicion of the camp was something he could *feel*.

"They know who I be," he said to the parson.

"O' course, you getting Rusty to sing that blame' song every chance you get."

"I doubt that was it." His eyes were on Royal's camp.

"Now don't you start any trouble," the parson said in alarm.

"I'll guarantee this . . . I'll start no more trouble than I can finish."

A while later, when big Betsy Cobb was ladling stew into an iron plate for him, she said: "Brother John, there's a story about this camp that you're that ornery, no-account, killing, robbing Comanche John, and I want ye to know I'm taking no belief in it."

"Thank-ee," said John. "Only I hear he ain't so bad. Steals from the rich to give to the poor. Confines his killin' strictly to varmints, Abolitionists, and that ilk."

He ate, wiped up the last bit of gravy on a biscuit, ate that, and dropped the plate back in the plunder box. Then he cut over through the river brush to the spot where he'd left his bed.

Suddenly he was aware of danger—a slight movement, a sound, a danger he seemed to *smell*. What caused him to dip his head and dive forward he never knew, but he *did*—and powder flame burst in his face, and there was a wind whip of lead passing, plucking at the crown of his black slouch hat.

He was face down in the clay dirt. He wanted to draw back and shoot, but he fought back the urge. The ambusher was only a dozen steps away, across a little gully, on slightly higher ground, waiting for his slightest movement.

He was there a quarter or half a minute that seemed much longer. He could hear men talking, coming from camp, wondering what the shot was. Then he heard a *crack* of brush on the river side and sensed that he was safe. Still cautious, drawing a Navy, he sat up and inspected the nick the bullet had put in his hat.

No one actually came to investigate. Someone was always shooting a grouse, or trying to stun one of those big Salmon River trout in shallow water. It was almost dark now, but across the gully, pressed in the soft clay ground, he found the ambusher's tracks—moccasin tracks, the toed-in moccasin tracks that meant only one man: Vogel.

He first moved his bed, then his horse, picketing the gunpowder for an easy getaway if one proved necessary. He inspected the loading of both Navies and put them back in their holsters, just so. That completed, he walked through the dark to the small fire where the renegades were broiling venison ribs and baking doughgods, wrapped snail-like around sticks and propped over the coals.

Hunkered, tending the cooking, were Belly River Bob and Moose Petley. Sanchez was a shadow and a shine of oily skin in the background, and in the middle of things, swaggering around on his double-jointed legs, was Vogel.

"You're damned right I kilt him," Vogel was braying, answering some doubt on the part of his hearers. "I was thar, waiting for him, and, when he came up and saw me . . . well!"

"You tell Royal?" Petley asked.

"Naw. Not yet. Don't want to interfere with his lovemakin'. That red-headed sprout was playing his banjo for her this afternoon, and she *liked* it. Royal will kilt that kid just like I kilt the Comanche."

Sanchez was looking into the shadows, the firelight showing on his teeth as he grinned. "Eh, *señor*, do you believe in ghosts?"

"What?" said Vogel.

John said: "Why, yes, here I be. What was it you were saying, about a man turning yellow when he runs face up against it?"

For a second Vogel's face was slack from shock and fear. Then he recovered and tried to bluster it out: "I warn't talking about *you*. I. . . ."

"You got mighty poor style with those guns of yours," John said. "And you be a Californy man, too. I hate to see a Californy man git vulgar with guns . . . pride, ye know, being a Californy man myself. So I decided it was up to me to give ye a lesson.

"For instance," John went on, "when ye draw, don't grip hard and jerk. Do it slow. Take your time. Make your arm sort of loose and lift that loose-going arm with your shoulder. I tell ye what, Vogel, let's both of us draw and I'll show ye what your mistake is."

"No." Vogel wanted to get away, but he was in the open and there was no cover for twenty feet. He took a step back, shaking his head hard. "No. You'd kill me if I drew. You're trying to get me to draw and kill me. But you don't dare kill me if I don't draw. They'll hang you. They will sure if you kill me."

"That's something else I'm talking about . . . lack of confidence. That's pizen to a gunman. Well, if you won't draw first, I'll have to draw for ye. Watch my right hand, now. See how I do it. Up, like this!"

He drew the right-hand Navy, but the hammer caught in the bottom of his jacket, and that pulled it free of his hand.

35

He made a grab for it and hit it instead, knocking it five or six feet away from him. He started for it, apparently off guard, and Vogel, thinking he saw his chance, jumped back straddle-legged and drew both guns.

They were out of the leather, but John, straightening with a half-slouched pivot, had drawn his left-hand Navy. He hesitated for a fragment of time. He gave the illusion of taking his sweet time while Vogel jerked his guns fast as a coiling snake.

The Navy exploded with a pencil of flame, spinning Vogel so one of his long legs seemed to wrap around the other. Vogel lunged with both guns exploding at his own boot toes and went down with his hat tumbling off and his face on top of the hat that was under him and he came against the ground.

John, without losing sight of the others, blew smoke from the muzzle of the Navy, and picked up his fallen gun.

"Thar, see what I mean? Jerked, muscles too tight. I been running into a mighty poor breed of gunmen lately. Mighty poor."

IV

"A MEETING"

From the safety of the river brush, John chawed and watched the camp. They were holding a meeting by the steps of Joe Woods's wagon where everyone was attempting to be heard at once. Finally Royal, by reason of his height and voice, took command and said there was only one course to follow with killers of John's cut, and that was hanging.

"Hang him? We got to catch him first!" called a man named Kippen. "I think he already run for it."

Royal said: "We're rid of him, then. So much the better!"

O'Donnell then tried to say that Vogel was a killer himself by his own account, and Royal started to shout him down, towering in anger as he always did when a man disagreed, but other men were heard demanding that O'Donnell be given his say, so Royal, with an effort, clamped his mouth shut and listened.

O'Donnell, halting and self-conscious now that everyone was looking at him, said: "He carried two guns. Men that carry two guns are looking for trouble."

Wally Snite said: "And how many pistols did the black-whiskered one carry?"

"Two. They were both looking for trouble. And they

found it. Anyhow, it wasn't one of our bunch that was killed."

They were fairly well divided, and a crowd has to be allied mighty strongly against a man before there's hanging, so John felt safe enough to come around by the parson's wagon for a better look-see.

"You got blood on your hands!" the Widow Cobb said, glimpsing him. "I don't know but what I'm shocked and grieved at you, Brother John. You killed a human being and you'll answer for it at Judgment."

"So'd young David have blood on his hands when he knocked down Goliath, but that didn't prevent him singing his psalms. Behold, woman, I carry my Navies to draw on the side o' righteousness and that's more'n I can say for *some* of the unregenerated varmints around here."

"Glory be, you may have some wisdom there. I don't cotton to gunfightin', but if it had to be, I'd rather it'd be that dirty, no-account, swaggering, cursing Ed Vogel than 'most anybody I know. Anyhow, we got to give him a Christian burial. We got to lay him out and comb him, and I wouldn't be surprised if we had to de-louse him."

"Lice don't stick with a dead man, Sister Betsy," said a small, tired-looking woman, Ambrose Stocker's wife. "That's a tried and true test for the dead. My mother's people were much afflicted with the rigid fits, and Grandmother Toston always tried 'em with a louse, and, if the louse crawled off, they were dead. They're the lower creatures, and they got a seventh instinct not known to man."

"When I'm rigid," said John, "you don't need to bother with the louse . . . you can just bury me."

"Oh," said the Widow Cobb, "why *couldn't* this have happened *yesterday* instead of tonight? Now everybody will be wanting to roll before sunup and the reverend will have no chance for a decent burial. Well, nothing can be done about it, I suppose. We'll just *have* to make out. It must needs be a nighttime service. They can be very nice. Very nice. I do wish we had plumes. They add *such* a touch. I wish the reverend would come over here and tell us if he intends to preach brimstone."

"That's what I like," said John. "Brimstone."

A third woman, Mrs. O'Donnell, said: "I don't care much for brimstone at a funeral. I think you ought to go easy on the dead, especially if there's relatives present."

John said: "I guess I was closer to Vogel than anybody else, knew him since 'Forty-Nine, both come from Pike County, ye got my consent."

They had caught sight of John, and there came Phelps and Stocker with a horse pistol and a shotgun respectively. John was now slightly apprehensive for he had no desire to be forced into trading shots with the emigrants.

"Put the guns down, boys," he said, ambling toward them, tired and dragging his jackboots. "I got no fight with you. I kilt a man, true. Kilt him in a gun duel. Self-defense. Why, they wouldn't even jail me for that in Illinoiz."

Stocker shouted. "You went over there on the prod, looking for him! You shot him down in cold blood."

"Who said?"

"Moose Petley, Belly River Bob, all of 'em."

"Oh, *them*." He wanted to retreat but those guns were on him. Many of the emigrants were fingering guns. He said: "Something else . . . something I didn't tell ye. He tried to ambush me. Yonder, by the river, around twilight. That was the shot ye all heered. I dove and it saved me. Thought he'd kilt me, he did."

Stocker laughed and said: "Oh, hell!"

There was other talk, low talk; nobody believed him. Wood was looking around, troubled, getting ready to mount the steps. Wood was a great one for democracy; he would put it to an open vote, and that might be bad. John started looking around to retreat when Rusty McCabe, with a frightened expression, climbed to the steps.

"Hold on, I saw it." Rusty did not look at Royal. He was scared of Royal, but he was talking anyway. His face looked white as a toadstool in the light, his freckles standing out. It was cold, but there was a shine of perspiration above his eyebrows. He went on: "We, I . . . I was over hunting for Lafe's gray mare, saw it all. Thought he was dead . . . John, I mean. Didn't know what to do. I came over here. I guess I was scared. I thought Vogel would kill me."

Royal shouted: "That's a plain lie! Look how they pal up together, him and John, him always singing that song."

Wood said in his quiet voice that carried so well: "Rusty! Was somebody with you?"

Rusty was unable to say no. He was looking across the heads of the crowd, and a second later, also frightened and sick, thirteen-year-old Veltis Smith crept into view.

"Yeah, I saw it, yeah." Veltis nodded his head very hard. In fright, with his long blond hair hanging over his face and his eyes shining through it, he looked idiotic. But he was telling the truth. No one could doubt he was telling the truth.

Wood said: "You have nothing to be afraid of. Was it like he said?"

"Yeah."

Royal said: "You believe *them?*" He tossed his head with a bitter laugh. He took off his beaver hat and rubbed his palm across his forehead. "Look at what you're believing . . . *them!*" And leaving them with his contempt, he went long-striding toward his wagon.

V

"NORTH FORK TRAIL"

As for the funeral, Betsy's worst fears were realized. The wagoners, already kept up late, were impatient for their beds and fewer than half of them came to the service. There was no coffin, of course, and no funeral really looks like a funeral without one. The parson was not up to his usual form, only drawing a few morals on the fate of the unregenerated, and not even touching on the weeping and the gnashing and the seven seas of sulphurous fire. It was all very anticlimactic after the excitement at Wood's wagon.

"Well, maybe it's for the best," the widow said. "I know it might sound peculiar to some, but I *am* relieved my husband, that sainted Mister Cobb, passed away on the Platte where we felt like we could take a decent time to bury him. It's my notion that there's nothing throws a crimp into a funeral like an over-hurried preacher."

It turned colder in the night, with a few crystals of snow. In the darkness of early morning, when the wagon train got into movement, the snow had stopped, but there were no stars, and gray clouds covered the mountains. The wagons pulled harder in the cold; the bumps of the rocky trail seemed to jar them worse. They camped again on the

41

Salmon, in thicker timber, with the mountains rising steeply from the narrow valley.

Next day the main stream was left behind, and they followed the North Fork. The road became narrow. Originally it was an Indian trail, later used by fur traders who found they could cross with two-wheeled carts, and next, with wagons, by the Mormon party in 1852, and by the Deer Valley settlers under Brighton three years later. Now, however, everyone seemed bound for the gold camps of Bannack and Hangtown, or coming over from the Snake River diggings, following the Lolo to Hell Gate, so several years might have passed since the last wagon had gone up this North Fork trail.

Windfalls continually blocked the way and had to be chopped out. There were slides and fallen boulders. In places the road was little better than a pack horse trail with the mountain on one side and the swift waters of the North Fork on the other, and wagons tilted so precariously that men had to hang to their uphill sides to weight them against capsizing.

There was no clustering of wagons at night; they camped in groups along the trail. Only a slight wind blew down the deep valley but with a feel of winter that made men turn their backs to it, and eat in the shelter of canvas, or inside the wagons.

"What the hell kind of a country you takin' us to?" Phelps said to Comanche John. "Winter come in September?"

"This is October in my calendar." John meant by his knees and hips, which became slightly lame after riding in the cold. "These mountain passes snow up early, but lower down, at the White Pine where ye be headed, I'd wager on some fine weather yet."

"But how long to get there? Oh, you don't need to fret . . . all you have to do is teepee in with the Injuns, I suppose . . . but we got to build some sort of shelter against the cold. What route you plan to guide us to the White Pine?"

"Only good way there is . . . up to Hell Gate, then east following the freight road on the Clark's, and then south again."

"North, and east, and back again. What kind of judgment is that? Why not cut across?"

"Maybe ye can fly across like an eagle?"

"There's a cut-across road by Big Hole Pass. How about that?"

"You been talking to Royal, ain't ye? Oh, I know he's been talking the Big Hole for days, trying to say my route is the long way around. It's long, all right, but it will git you thar."

He could see that Phelps didn't believe him. Phelps, Stocker, and Snite were strong for Royal and it would be a fine ruckus trying to hold the train together once they reached the Big Hole turn-off.

He found the parson in his wagon, shivering, trying to start a fire with damp wood in his little Santa Fé stove. A tallow dip, a bit of wool lying in a can of half-congealed bear grease, gave the crowded, tunnel-like interior of the wagon a flickering, ruddy glow.

"We be headed for trouble at the Big Hole turn-off," John said to the old man. "I'll bet that rangy woolly wolf has talked half the wagons into turning east."

"Royal? He ain't convinced Wood. Nor Lela, because she'll stick with her pa. And where Lela goes, Royal will go. He's enamored o' her."

"But you sure Wood will stick fast to going by Hell Gate?"

"He'll go. Don't you worry about Wood. He's got an uncommon level head for a Pike's Peaker."

The parson was suffering from rheumatics, so John stayed with him and helped with his work. Next day the train moved very slowly as the trail steepened. At particularly steep pitches the tandem wagons had to be disconnected and pulled one at a time. After each pitch the grade seemed to level a little, and the worst appeared to be over, but always the next pitch would be even steeper.

They commenced to find snow in the shelter of stones and trees. The clouds that for three days had hung low hiding the mountaintops raised to reveal a new land, a land of towering peaks and ridges, a wilderness of rock already deep in snow. The mountains extended range after range, apparently forever, making more than one of the wagoners feel his own insignificance, placing a cold knot in his middle, this plunging into a cold and inhospitable land.

At a meeting that night Royal produced a map cut from a St. Louis paper some years before and now ready to fall apart at the folds from long carrying. It showed no route at all to the Bitterroot, but two-thirds to the crest they were struggling toward was a heavy, double line pointing east marked **Big Hole Pass**. The double line ran on, straight to Deer Lodge Valley, and at the bottom was the legend: **Good Wagon Road**.

"Now he would be a guide for us," said John, "the editor of that Saint Louis paper. Look down here . . . he's got his road going up the wrong side of the Salmon."

His words slightly discredited the map, but the sentiment for turning off was still well divided. Later, at the wagon, the parson said they'd have to do something and John answered: "I'll do *something*. I'll let 'em run their chicken crates off the brink of hell if that's their choice."

"No, John. I promised to guide 'em to Fort Hall, and from there I promised to furnish a dependable guide the rest of the way, and that's *you*."

John got the parson set for the night and left with black slouch hat pulled down against the wind. There was a light in Wood's wagon, and the moving shadows of many men were silhouetted against its canvas top. So they were having another powwow.

"T'hell with 'em," he muttered.

Wagons filled the trail leaving scant room for a man to walk without climbing rocks and timber. Snow had settled in, ankle-deep in places, and he could feel it strike cold through a rent in the instep of his right boot.

"I'm in damn' poor shape for winter," he muttered. "No boots, no grubstake, no fat on my horse and none on me, neither. By grab, this is my last winter of this. I'm going to find me a Blackfeet gal, snug teepee, somebody to look to my comfort. Plenty buffaler jerky, plenty dried choke-cherry. Worse things in the world."

He was still muttering, getting his jacket tied against the cold, when he noticed the two saddle horses hitched on the lee side of Wally Snite's wagon. One of them was the big, bald-faced sorrel that Petley liked to ride, and, although it was too dark to be sure, he thought the other belonged to Little Tom.

They were gone most of the time, those two, leaving Bob and the Mexican to drive the big, almost empty Pittsburgh wagon and herd the dozen head of saddle stock that formed Royal's outfit. He couldn't remember seeing them at all since the second morning on the North Fork.

He kept talking to himself because talking seemed to help keep him warm. "Scouting for Injuns. *Their* story. Makin' friends with Injuns, more like."

That last was a bad thought. Since the Cayuse War the Indians this side of the mountains had not been so bold. North, toward Palouse country, even the prospectors were going in parties of fifteen or more, every man with pistol and carbine! And this outfit pulled by horses and mules! Nothing an Indian will fight harder to get than a horse, unless maybe it's a gun.

He drew up, seeing a girl and man ahead of him, half concealed in the shadow of a supply wagon. They stood very still, and it took him a second to realize that the girl was Lela Wood, and the boy Rusty.

John put them at ease, saying: "Just been up tucking that danged old preacher in bed. Pining away, he is. Just too many funerals and not enough weddings. Turning morbid. Nothing I could do about it short of marrying that Widda Cobb, and it wouldn't be the same as marrying young folks."

"Oh!" said Lela, acting as though she wanted to stop him, but, of course, really she didn't—gals always acted that way.

He pretended to have an interest in the camp and looked all around. Then he sidled close to Rusty and said from the side of his mouth: "Go ahead and ask her. See what she says."

After a tongue-tied moment Rusty said—"Lela. . . ."—and bogged down.

"Oh, Rusty," she said, on the verge of tears and a moment later she had her head on his shoulder.

John plodded on, saying: "I just go along doing good deeds beside the way, gittin' business for the parson."

He tended the gunpowder, finding a park-like area a quarter mile from camp where the grass was still untouched. He picketed the pony and, using his hat, rubbed all over his coat, thinking how just a little extra attention paid off, keeping an animal in shape so he'd be able to make the long travel someday and save a man's life.

He put his saddle and bed under cover and went back down the mountain, digging in his boot heels and holding onto rocks to keep from sliding. Soon he heard voices through the trees below and knew that the powwow had broken up. The voices were excited. He let one group of men pass, and stopped O'Donnell when he came along.

"What be it?" he asked.

"Oh, you, John. The two men just came back from the mountains. They were across the Big Hole Pass."

"I suppose they found pavement like in Saint Loo?"

"There's been a gold strike."

"Whar?"

"They called it the Proctor Diggings."

"Oh. Waal, that's not new. Fact is, I was to the Proctor not two months ago. Narrow gulches, five or six of 'em, in among the timber. Pay streak generally couple o' feet wide. Coarse stuff and good . . . gold's always good . . . only them that made the first rush to Proctor hogged it all. There be some claims up on the mountain, hard rock, three Chineemen making wages pounding up quartz in hand mortars. *Chinee* wages, that is, nothing to interest a human being. You mean that's the big news?"

O'Donnell was already calling the others, saying here was more information about the Proctor Diggings and that this wasn't so good. They gathered and listened skeptically, for John's news was bad, and most of them were experiencing the glow of millionaires.

Ambrose Stocker came pushing through, saying: "Just why are you trying to keep us to this side away from those diggings? How you greasing your skillet in this? You think you can cut a bigger strike of that gravel for yourself?"

John, with a cold anger settling in him, waved men from his way and took a step toward Stocker, who retreated.

"Don't you try that on me!" Stocker said with apprehension tightening his voice. "I got friends here. You won't git away with gunning me down like you did Vogel."

"Stocker, I been up and down this country for a year or three and I been much amazed at how little trouble a man gits himself into by keeping a good lead string on his tongue."

"Well, all right, but I'll leave it to Lafe and to Dilworth if I didn't say that you'd try to blow cold air on it the first chance you got."

"Why didn't they stay if it was so good . . . Petley and Little Tom?"

"They staked their gravel."

"What you aim on doing . . . just give up the White Pine and go to mining?"

More and more were gathering around, some of them women, and it was for them he intended his words about the White Pine, but he soon learned that they were even more hungry for sudden wealth than their menfolk.

Mrs. Dilworth, who dressed like and did the work of a man, said: "If I thought there was a chance for money, I'd give up the White Pine. I'd give it up in a minute." She thrust out her hands, palms up. "Look at 'em. Calluses like a man's. No nigger ever worked harder than me, but I never heered no Abolitionist beating his drum to free *me* from slavery. I ought to have 'em half soled like you would a pair of boots. Born in a shanty not fitten for a hawg. No floor, rain come through, married at thirteen. Oh, my men tried hard enough . . . both of 'em. Lord knows *I* tried hard enough. Slave all year for the locusts and green worms to eat up. Borry money and have the bank foreclose. Move to Kansas, scrimp and save and build three years on a house, and just when you get a roof over your head, and a floor instead of the dirt, then the slavery people burn you out, your own people. Look at that shoe! Home-tanned leather soled with buffalo back. A slave in the field don't wear nothing like that. No stockings, even. And what's at the White Pine but more of the same? So if we git a chance for the gold, a chance to git and be able to buy a few of the better things, I say let's take that chance. Let's head for the Proctor."

Sobered by the speech, John said: "Maybe you'd be better off going for the gold, I ain't saying, and that's up to you. But if ye want the gold, turn your wagons smack around and roll back to the Bannack Pass. Head up the Ruby. That's the country for gold, and silver, too, if you're willing to drill and hammer. The point is . . . you're either miners or you're farmers. It's mighty hard to be both at the same time."

Wally Snite, hiding in the background, jeered: "And by morning we'll be fighting over a pass that never was, and he'll be gone to grab the best of the Proctor Diggings for himself."

John chose to ignore him as he would ignore a barking terrier. "Tell ye what . . . it's still a pull to Big Hole turn-off. Why not send a couple of your men over to look at the Proctor for themselves?"

Snite and Stocker were willing to jeer at that, too, but it appealed to the better heads among them and just then Joe Wood walked up. Informing himself of the dispute, he said: "Very well, let's have a couple of volunteers."

The only one anxious to go was Snite, and few were willing to trust him, so the decision was put off until morning.

John wanted to listen to the temper of those who had less to say, so he hunted pitch pine along the hill for the parson. He was returning with an armload of resinous bark when Mrs. Dilworth suddenly appeared and said: "Say, Wood has been looking all over for you."

"Whar is he?" John asked, putting down the wood.

The woman said: "At his wagon, I suppose."

There was candlelight inside, and he could see the shadow of someone moving around, so he rapped. Wood said— "Come in."—and John opened the end gate door and climbed through.

"What were ye wanting?" John asked.

Wood had taken off his heavy wool shirt, apparently getting ready for bed. Lela was not there.

"I didn't want anything," Wood said.

"Said ye did . . . Missus Dilworth."

"How'd that fool woman get anything like that in her head?"

John chuckled and said: "Gold fever . . . it makes 'em see things. Now, understand, I'm not talking for the Proctor, but actually I think most folks would be happier starving to death digging for gold than getting medium fat on a farm. With a farm you know ye won't get far, but a miner always has a billion dollars just ahead of his shovel. And not very damned far ahead, either."

"Yes, I suppose." Wood looked very tired. He was not a rugged man—mentally, perhaps, but not physically. "You've had a pretty tough time with these men. I understand. I suppose I understand better than anyone else. But once we get to the other side, once the road eases out, you'll find they're not unreasonable."

"Provided we git to the other side. Won't if they vote for the Big Hole. Listen. I've been up thar. Not from here, but from yonder, traveling this way. Anyhow, I had a look at her as far as the crest. Maybe you could get a wagon over. But it's a cliff route, a switchback route. If there's deep snow, or there's been a rock slide. . . ."

"*They* were across it."

"Petley and Little Tom?" In his disgust, John was tempted to spit tobacco juice on the floor.

"You don't trust them?"

"Do you? They're renegades, back-shooters, the worst. Why ain't they at the gold camps? I'll tell ye . . . because even Bannack and Hangtown can't stomach 'em. They'd stretch a rope down there, you take my word for it."

Joe Wood moved around, scratching his body through

his knit, woolen undershirt and looking John in the eyes. "What do you think of Royal?"

"You know that. Why in hell did you let him jine up?"

"Asked to. Knew the country. How did I know the parson's guide would ever show up when you weren't at Fort Hall?"

"Ye know what I think Royal's got on his mind? Robbery! He'll strand ye in the snow, and you'll have to abandon and go to the low country for winter, and then he'll pack horse your supplies down and sell them in Proctor and Mucho Gulch and those other far back camps where an ounce of gold trades for ten pounds of flour."

"Oh, no, no! You're most definitely wrong about that."

"It war done before, yonder in Oregon, wagon train coming across the Malheur attacked by Injuns, only they waren't Injuns, but white men in brown ochre and feathers, with a help from some guides with the train. I tell ye, thar's no crime too low or devilish but a white man ain't tried it sometime since the gold rush of 'Forty-Nine, and I say that's quite a record in just fourteen short years."

Wood was listening, trying to hear something over the sound of John's voice. John paused and listened, too. It was not a sound, but a tremble of the wagon. John instinctively moved into the shadows with hands dangling below the butts of his Navies. Wind rustled a bit of loose canvas against the wagon box and the thought came to him that was what it had been, a push of wind down the valley, making the wagon shake.

Wood, too, dismissed it from his mind and turned as if to reach for something on the table, and at that instant the air was rocked by flame and explosion. The gunshot had burst from only a few feet away, from the drawstring window at the forepart of the wagon.

John instinctively drew and spun away. He fired both pistols, aiming below the window, hoping for a lucky shot when the man tried to escape. Wood had been knocked across the table. He hung, bent over at the abdomen, his arms dangling. The candle did a crazy dance along the edge in its holder and fell, blinking out on the floor.

"Wood!" John said, groping for him. He was no longer on the table. He fell, striking across the side of John's right leg. He hit the floor with a dead man's loose, limp *thud* that shook the wagon.

Powder fumes were thick beneath the low, curved ceiling. Holding his breath, John dropped to one knee and tried for his pulse, not finding it. New voices were coming that way, voices of men apparently on every side rushing closer.

One was Wally Snite. No one could mistake Snite's magpie voice and he was going at it as never before: "It's Wood. That dirty killer. Comanche John was in there with him! They were quarreling about sending men to Proctor. I think he killed him."

"Who?"

"Wood. I think he's dead. That dirty killer . . . we should have hung him. I said we should have hung him."

There was no waiting. John left Wood's body. He did not even get to his feet. He merely slid backward, boots first, and dropped to the ground through the end gate door.

Men were bearing down on him through darkness from up and down the road. He slid beneath the wagon. There, with one Navy drawn, he took a few seconds to estimate his chances. On one side, the bank dropped off across rocks the size of gravestones to the swift water of the North Fork. On the other, toward the mountainside where his horse waited, was a shoulder of ground, very steep-faced and almost bare at its crest.

He moved farther under the wagon. He could hear the men very close. He could see the lower halves of their bodies as they ran up and stopped, not knowing where to go next, each fearing to be the first inside the wagon. Men were so close he could have touched their legs. He remained crouched, his back against the under frame, cursing through his teeth.

From a distance came Royal's voice: "Anybody gone inside the wagon?"

No answer.

Then Dilworth: "Damn it, he might be waiting in there. . . ."

Lela was running up around the upgrade wagons, crying: "My dad, my dad . . . !"

Poor little gal! John thought. *It won't help your sorrows, gal, but I'll git him for you. Before I'm through, I'll git that bushwhacker.*

Someone, braver than the rest, entered the rear door of the wagon above him. John moved on, into the open near the front wheel. He almost rubbed shoulders with a passing man. The darkness saved him. He walked, just walked slowly, forcing himself to go slowly.

In the uphill distance Moose Petley was shouting: "Hey, where's his horse? That's where he'll be . . . after his horse!"

John was away from one cluster of wagons, not yet to the next. Thirty feet farther was a trail that would take him up the mountains, but a running man suddenly loomed hugely in front of him and they collided. It was Stocker, and, as he staggered for balance, Stocker recognized him.

"Covered!" John said. "Drop your gun. That's it. Pistol, too. Now walk!"

At gunpoint he took Stocker up the mountain, through timber, to the little open space where the gunpowder waited, ears cocked, lifting his picket string.

"Now, fare ye well," said John. "Git! And ye can brag to your children and your children's children how ye once looked into the Navy of the one and gen-u-wine Comanche John and lived to tell the tale."

VI

"CAPTURED!"

Comanche John rode through timber, following a dim deer track along the mountainside, taking his time, letting the pony pick his way, bending the pine branches away, singing in a soft monotone a new stanza that Rusty had picked up in Fort Hall:

> **Thar's a forty-dozen highwaymen**
> **'Twixt Denver and the sea,**
> **But I sing of old Comanche John**
> **The toughest one thar be.**
> **He robbed the bank, he robbed the stage,**
> **He robbed the Yuba mail,**
> **And he left his private graveyards**
> **All along the Bannack trail.**

"By grab," he said, "that's a fine verse. A beautiful verse. I'd like to find the muleskinner that wrote that verse and banquet him with likker."

He built a tiny brush lean-to, cut spruce with his Bowie, and slept rolled in his robes until dawn and the cold awakened him. All day, from one remote pinnacle and another he watched the wagons move along, and he saw them camp

55

where the rough tracks of the Big Hole trail forked to the east.

He wondered if Royal would prevail, now that there was no one except the parson to oppose him. Thought of the parson troubled him, and so he did not strike out for the gold camps as he might have done. Instead, he shot a grouse, roasted it over a tiny fire, and ate it half raw with a chew of tobacco for dessert.

He slept and rode back at dawn to find the outfit still camped, wagons being repaired, stock grazing the bottoms. Later he saw Petley and Little Tom ride off toward the east, and a hunch made him follow them.

He kept them in sight for an hour. After that he trailed through the light snow. Toward evening two other horses joined them. A peculiar something about the new set of prints made him dismount for a closer inspection. These horses were unshod, that is, their hoofs were covered by rawhide stockings, heat-shrunk to such hardness that even the mountain snow and damp did not loosen them, Indian horses, Palouse or Bannock.

He trailed, and darkness slowed him. A bleak ridge of solid stone rose on one side, and the cliff walls of a gulch lay on the other, so their only possible course lay through a saddle to the east. He rode on, picking up the tracks again miles later.

He was now near the crest of the range with the Big Hole country dropping away before him, and his nostrils, sharpened by the autumn freshness, detected the odor of wood smoke. It guided him to the brink of a little cirque-like valley containing a lake and meadow, an L-shaped log house, some corrals, and a horse shed.

It surprised him to find such a place so deep in the wilderness until he realized that this was Desette's Rendezvous where in the old days of the beaver trade a representative of the S.L.&Y. Company came each year to trade with the Indians crossing over from the Salmon River.

Lights glowed in two brownish-amber squares—windows of the cabin covered with parchment or oiled wrapping paper.

He turned back, and at a distance of a mile by a trickle of gulch water he found grass for his horse, unsaddled and picketed him. Then he went down, through timber, coming on the house from the corrals.

A grease-dip light was burning in a closed end of the shed, and men were talking in the Chinook jargon. He peeped through a hole in the chinking and saw five men, all of them half-breeds or Indians, cross-legged or sprawled on the earthen floor, playing a knife and stick game for gold coins. He had seen none of them before.

He went on, finding shadow, and paused at the back of the house. Inside, he could hear the dull mutter of voices, but no word was audible. Wary for a sentry, he circled and walked along the front, beneath a pole awning, past one of the parchment-covered windows, to the door.

The door was closed, but it was whip-sawed lumber, warped and ill-fitting, and he could see and hear. One of the men was Moose Petley. By a fireplace stood a gaunt old Indian with hair cropped like a white man. Two other men, Indians or half-breeds, stood with their backs turned, and there were more, how many he did not know.

A soft whisper of footsteps told him of someone's approach from the direction of the horse shed, and, forced to a quick decision, he looked around for concealment. There was none handy, but the porch roof was supported by substantial timbers, the lower braces running solidly from pillars to the house. He reached, chinned himself up and over one of them, and crouched on one knee with head and back bent against the ceiling as the man came in sight and walked directly beneath him, so close his breathing was audible. He was a short, very broad man, and no Indian about him, just plain renegade. John checked his own breathing till he went inside.

This was a fine place from which to listen and watch, provided he could make himself comfortable. He turned himself, careful for balance, braced himself on one hand and knee, and lay full length. The timber was a scant six inches wide, but it had been squared, and lying, not moving in the slightest, he was able to stay in balance. With his hat rolled up to cushion the side of his head, he listened.

They were planning an attack two days hence, three at most. But it evolved slowly, bit by bit, and each bit was the subject of protracted wrangling.

He had been full length on the timber for hours. He was cold, his feet had gone dead, but he dared not move for fear of giving himself away to a couple of the Indians close inside the door before the last of the plan had evolved.

Then unexpectedly the meeting broke up. It was getting daylight, and they came outside, Moose Petley and the scarfaced Indian, Little Tom, and the renegade white man, and five others.

Petley and Tom disappeared toward the corrals, and minutes later he heard the sound of hoofs departing. The Indians and half-breeds had stopped directly below him and all were talking at once.

"Good!" one of the half-breeds said. "Big skookum, eh? Damn' right. Plenty horse, plenty gun. Maybe plenty grub, too, sell 'em for good price in a mining town? What you think?"

The scarfaced one made a sign for him to talk lower, but John knew now that they planned to go along with Royal only so far, to attack the wagon train, yes, and, when the time came, to double-cross him, for these were not ordinary Indians on a horse raid. They were hardened renegades who long ago had learned the wealth of the white man.

He waited for them to go away, but it was morning now and they stayed outside. At last, however, only three were left and those at the far end of the porch arguing in a tongue he did not understand. It was getting brighter by the moment. He was just overhead, so close he could smell the smoky, Indian tan of their buckskin shirts when they passed beneath him to the door, and it was improbable that he would go much longer undetected. His best chance was to move now, despite the men on the porch, to escape with aid of his Navies, to gamble that his horse could outlast pursuit.

He checked his guns and tried to raise himself, swing his legs over, grab the beam, and lower himself. He was unbalanced, with paralysis holding him. He experienced a long second of nightmare helplessness, muscles congealed, and he was falling.

He managed to break his fall on outflung hands. He tried to roll and draw his Navies as the men in surprise looked at him. He could not get off his elbows and knees, and of a sudden men were all around him, all shouting questions, no one realizing where he had come from.

He said the only thing he could think of: "Long riding . . . stiffened me. Whar's Petley? Little Tom?" He managed, with pain, to get to his feet. He stamped his feet as, with a million prickles of fire, life was forced back through them.

The scarfaced one—he was one-eyed with the right side of his face from cheek bone to forehead cleft from an old tomahawk wound—came up and cried: "Where you from?"

"Royal."

"I don't savvy you. Don't see you no time."

"Waal, ye see me now. Whar's Petley?"

"He go, long time."

"Then I'll just have to bring ye the word myself. It's off. The raid is off. Crawford and his volunteers . . . you savvy Crawford?" He knew by their expressions that, indeed, they savvied Crawford, whose group of volunteers had lately cleared the Bannocks and Cheyennes from the South Pass. "Many men. Mountain guns. Cannon, that is. German repeaters."

The scarface said: "Crawford south, many sleeps."

"All right. I'll not argue with ye. It's your grave if ye want to fill it. Done my part. Brought ye the warning like Royal asked. So now I'll just be gittin' back."

"No," said the scarface. "You stop."

John saw an Indian reaching for his Navies and saying— "No ye don't!"—started to spin away, but he ran his forehead against something cold and hard. He stiffened. He turned his head slowly and looked down the barrel of a Jager rifle.

The scarface with a crafty look in his one eye said: "You wait, maybe you sneak up, listen? Maybe not. We send, find out."

They held him prisoner in a room with thick log walls that had served as the powder lock-up in fur trade days. It had no window, but he was able to judge the passage of day by the glints of light through the shake roof high above.

The door was held by a heavy bar on the outside. The pole flooring was loose, merely flattened on two sides and laid into place, but the room had its own rock foundation as a precaution against a fire creeping beneath to the powder kegs. The walls had been hewn smooth, the logs set flush one against the other, leaving no place for a finger or toehold, and the heavy pole members of the roof would be immovable anyway. It was an excellent prison. He sat with his back against a wall, chawed, and waited.

He could hear the Indians arguing horses. He learned by listening that the scarfaced one was Kinepah. John had heard a great deal about Kinepah. Kinepah was one of the Palouse chiefs in on the Steptoe massacre of 1858. He had escaped later from the Indian defeat at Four Lakes and had been on the loose ever since.

If that was Kinepah, then he guessed that the younger Palouse was Deerskin Shirt, and that the oldest man, the taciturn full-blood with the roached hair was Three Horse, who had been in trouble with white men since the Cayuse War back in 1848, which was a year before John first came West.

"What a fine crew Royal has tied himself up to," he muttered, talking to keep himself company. "Why, these renegades will use him, and they'll end by riding off with his hair and his beaver hat!"

VII

"ONE LAST WISH"

In a brief service, as a wind chilled the emigrants, the parson officiated at the burial of Joe Wood. The wagons then pulled on, leaving his grave as they had left others on the long haul from Kansas. Courteous and sympathetic, Royal came to Lela, holding his hat across his breast, and asked with humble earnestness for the privilege of driving her wagon, and she consented.

She had not seen Rusty since the night before. At first she was bitter, then apprehensive, but later, as Royal drove the wagon and she had a chance to talk to the others, she heard hints of proof that he had ridden off with Comanche John. When Mrs. Stocker said it was a fact that they had been seen together, she believed it.

That night, an hour before sundown, the lead wagons came to a halt at a fork in the road where Belly River Bob had already built a fire and was warming himself.

"There she is, the road to the Big Hole," he said, pointing at the crooked, narrow trail that branched off to follow a small creek to their right. "Road to the gold camp. If you're not satisfied with Proctor gold, why, it'll still save you ten days to the White Pine."

They held a meeting with Stocker in charge and voted three to one for Big Hole. The parson, his warning unheeded, retired to his wagon to brood, and there Betsy Cobb found him with a second bit of news—the wagon train had voted to lay over the next day for grass and repairs, and Royal had announced that Lela had consented to become his wife. The parson, low from misery, was able only to hold his head and speak of fate.

It warmed very slightly next day. In the morning everyone worked putting wagons and gear in shape. In the afternoon, Mrs. Shallerbach and Mrs. Stocker took charge of the wedding and moved everything out of the Stocker wagon save a stand they decorated with their best fancywork, making an altar. While this was going on, Betsy Cobb appeared again at the parson's wagon.

She stood with hands on hips and said: "You ain't takin' a part in this wedding, are you?"

The parson said in resignation: "It ain't of my choosing."

"He kilt Joe Wood. Her own father."

"Of that we got no proof."

"Then you mean you'll marry 'em, Parson?"

"Alas, it's out of my hands. Who am I to struggle ag'in' fate?"

"You make me sick," she said, and stomped through the door.

The parson sat with his head in his hands while the fire in his stove died and twilight settled in the wagon. A rap sounded at the end gate door and he said—"Come in."—without looking up.

It was Mrs. Dilworth, dressed in men's clothes as usual. She looked gaunt and shaky.

"I had my hand in something terrible," she blurted out. "I did. I'm certain of it. I had my hand in murder."

The parson showed life. "Whose? Joe Wood's?"

"Yes. I was going to my wagon when Wally Snite . . . I never did trust him . . . I never trusted a man with pale eyes. . . ."

"What about Snite?"

"He said Joe Wood wanted to see John, so I told him, and they kilt him. I'm sure of it. They kilt him and laid it to John. I had my hand in murder. Why am I so sure? I'll tell you . . . because, if John wanted to kill him, would he have waited till Wood sent for him?"

The parson questioned her, but she had no proof.

"Don't you believe it?" she asked.

"Yes, I believe it, but would anybody else believe it? You go along and say nothing. I got to think about what to do."

The parson did think about it, and about himself, alone in his weakness. His first object was to stop the wedding. So he took to his bed and moaned. It was half an hour before one of the Orham kids heard him and went for help. Help came in the person of Betsy Cobb, who begged him to recognize her, to rise up for just one second and say so before he slipped over to Beulah Land.

The parson gasped for Lela Wood. The Orham kid sped off for her, and she came running, holding her borrowed wedding dress up away from the juniper.

"He's nigh gone," whispered Betsy Cobb, meeting her at the door. "Oh-h, I could see it coming. And I talked to him so, only two hours past. Oh-h! How can I ever forgive myself?"

"Parson!" Lela said on knees beside his bed.

"Who is it?" gasped the parson. "I heard the voice of an angel. Be I in heaven already?"

"You aren't going to die, Parson. You aren't!"

"Oh, yes, child! But I'll be a happy corpse. I will, now that you're here to promise me one thing. . . ."

"You're not." She looked up and saw Betsy and two other women just arrived, standing there. "Get some water heated. Heat up some stones. Blankets! And some whiskey. Is there any left?"

The parson said: "No use wasting likker on me. My earthly race is run. In my Father's house thar is many mansions, as the Good Book says, and I'll soon be trading this here ornery old prairie schooner for one of 'em."

She held his hand and whispered: "No, no."

Ague seized him and he shook all over, almost knocking off the quilts. "One last wish. It's for you, gal!"

"Yes!"

"I had an awful premonition. Don't go through with that wedding. Don't let any captain of any wagon train marry you after I'm gone, neither. I had a vision. Balls of fire and lakes of brimstone descending on this wagon train I seen if you did. Corpses and charred remains. Promise me you'll not get married until you get to the White Pine."

"I won't, Parson, I won't!"

"Ah," sighed the parson, and subsided with hands folded across his breast.

"Is he gone? Is he gone?" asked the Widow Cobb. "Glory to his sainted memory, is he gone? Do you reckon we ought to lay him out in his old black serge, or would you say his frock coat and gaiters? And a coffin! I say this time we must have a coffin."

The parson, with one eye open, whispered: "Don't rush me, Sister Cobb. Don't rush me."

The wedding was postponed. All night, with women hovering close, the parson clung to life.

VIII

"BIRDS ON THE WING"

At the moment the parson was gasping his last request to Lela Wood, Comanche John was seated in the darkness of the old powder room, chewing and spitting, still listening to the interminable Indian argument concerning horses. Then, to busy himself, he once more groped the room with the thought of escape.

The flooring again interested him. The rock foundation of the room was a hopeless barrier, but something else occurred to him. It made him spit hard, and chuckle, and say: "Why, damn me, yes!" He could move some of the poles near the door, lie flat on the ground with the poles over him, and present an empty room to the eyes of the first man who came to look for him.

He had to lie on his back, full length, and in that position it was not easy to replace the pole flooring over him, but he did it, and settled himself for a long wait. The ground was cold, but not uncomfortable, and much superior to his beam of the night before. He even dozed a little.

He awakened with a start, hearing voices at a new pitch and realizing that the messenger had returned from seeing Dave Royal. Soon he felt the jar of approaching moccasined feet, the scrape of the bar, the sound of the door being pulled open. With his eye at a crack between the poles he saw a man with a rifle aimed, peering around the room. It was the Palouse he assumed to be Deerskin Shirt.

"Ho!" said Deerskin Shirt, staying clear of the door, swinging his double pistol around at the blackness. "Come on, see chief."

John did not move the tiniest muscle, he did not breathe, he did not even blink. After a few seconds, Deerskin Shirt risked sticking his head inside. He suddenly realized that the room was empty. He looked all along the walls, above at the ceiling. He came then with long steps and stopped in the middle of the room.

The Indian's back was turned. Moving carefully, deliberately, John lifted the poles and sat up. One of the poles made a *thud,* and Deerskin Shirt started around, but John sprang and had him by the back of the jacket with his left arm bent around his throat.

The Indian was off balance for a second, then he tried to dump John over his head, but John was ready for the maneuver. It was a silent struggle across the room; the Indian was young, tough, and quick, but he was unable to break the power of the bent arm that cut off his breath.

They fell to the floor and John still held him, waiting as his struggles became futile, and then waiting a while yet. He let go then, picked up the double-barreled pistol, a smooth-bore loaded with buckshot, checked its percussion caps, and stepped from the door.

He was in a short hallway. He still had to go through the big room, and there were men there, six of them.

He walked up very quietly. A candle stood above the fireplace; rifles leaned against the wall; rifles lay on the table; his own Navies were also on the table, still in their holsters, belts wrapped around them. The one-eyed Kinepah had his back to him, talking in the Palouse tongue, gesturing his thoughts out in the sign language and all watching him.

John did not hurry. He walked to the table and picked up the Navies, put them under his left arm, the double-pistol aimed.

Then one of them saw him and raised a yell, but John froze them with the twin barrels of the pistol and moved to the door.

"Bird's on the wing," he said. "Savvy white talk? Waal, I wager ye savvy *gun* talk." He waved the pistol. "Some don't savvy white talk, and some don't savvy Injun, but the language of buckshot they understand even in Chinee."

One of the half-breeds had ducked from sight and, crawling, tried to come up from under the table with a rifle where John met him with a blast of shot that turned him over and laid him on his back. They were all after their guns, then, but John was through the door. He turned and fired again into the mass of them. The scarface was in the lead, just bringing his rifle up, and John flung the empty pistol, its five pounds of metal catching him squarely across the nose, clubbing him to the floor.

John covered the porch in five running strides and found shadow in trees. Bullets roared around him, cut fragments of bark, pounded dirt that stung the backs of his thighs. He slowed to a heavy trot, buckling on the Navies. His jackboots were not made for running. It was a temptation to pull them off and carry them and run in his bare feet. He kept going, crossed the little valley, and was at last on the steep mountain slope. With lungs bursting for air, he lay on the first crest, resting and getting his wind.

A bullet winged close, followed by a crack of explosion, stirring pebbles a dozen feet away. He crawled from view, stood, went on. He crossed the ridge and dropped down toward the depression where his horse waited.

"You're still here, pony," he said, breathing deeply, getting on the saddle.

He could hear pursuit, the *thud* of hoofs. He mounted and rode up the depression, over a small flank of the mountain through timber, bending branches away, keeping them from his face. No sound of pursuit now. He had just reached for his plug of tobacco, thinking he was shut of them, when suddenly he realized they had circled and were coming in on him from two sides.

He urged the gunpowder to a gallop, recklessly downhill, across rocks, through close-growing lodgepole. Bullets chased him. He kept at a trot and walk around the upper edge of timber with the giant slide rock of the ridge above. Ahead of him lay a black chasm, and leading upward among rock spires large as churches was a crooked little trail.

He had no choice; he followed it. He dismounted and helped the gunpowder as it steepened. The trail petered out. It had come to a blind end, to a dozen blind ends. He hid the horse among rocks and went back down, digging his boot heels into the steepness, sliding on the seat of his pants.

He saw them coming, gray shapes against the dark timber, drew down with a Navy, and fired. It was a miss at long range, but close enough to send them back and make them attempt to close in on him from the sides, and all night he kept on the move, saving his bullets, anticipating each tricky maneuver.

Dawn came, and it was very quiet. He climbed high and looked down. No movement anywhere. Still fearing ambush, he found a crooked hidden way for half a mile where a trail led him into what the night before had looked like a chasm, actually a very deep gulch. The trail led him down and down into the shadows. After a mile of twisting and turning he reached the bottom where an icy little stream flowed.

He rode, taking his time, forced to take his time. On the high flanks of the mountains the sun was bright, but he rode through deep shadows. He looked for a cut-across route to the Big Hole trail, but now he was hemmed in on both sides by peaks. It was midday before a trail took him up from the gulch, around the mountain. He crossed smaller gulches, topped a minor divide, and there, far across a deep and broad creek valley, he saw the moving shapes of wagons.

The sun was very bright. It was melting the snow, giving a green tint to the grass, making the tops of the wagons look spotless, like a picture with the dark mountain timber beyond.

He went on at an easy pace and was startled to hear his name called. He reined around and saw someone riding toward him, bareback, bareheaded, guiding his pony with a rope hackamore. It took him a couple of seconds to realize it was Rusty, and he was hurt.

He had been wounded on the head; he had bled a great deal; his hair was a solid mass of hardened blood. A purplish bruise extended down his left temple across his cheek; his eye was swollen shut. He carried his right arm in a peculiar manner close against his stomach.

"Lad, what the devil?"

"It was that night, that same night they laid in wait."

"For you? Who laid in wait?"

"I think Belly River Bob. He come up behind me, it was so quick, and next thing I knew I was down among the rocks. I don't know. I knew he was above, waiting for me to move, so I just laid there. Finally I crawled away among the rocks. Daylight before I could walk. Dizzy. Broke my arm. I followed the wagon train, but Sanchez was rear sentry. He'd have killed me. Finally I did coax this horse, Lafe's horse." Then he said defensively, angrily, raising his voice: "You think I'm a coward. I'm not. I'll git a gun and go back after those. . . ."

"No, now! You think because you git scared you're a coward? It's what a man does in spite of being scared tells whether he's a coward. Ye know, this is a bull-moose country you're growing to manhood in. It's the wild Nor'west, and that ain't exactly Ioway."

A movement far across and below caught John's restless eyes, stopping them, stopping his jaw from revolving around his tobacco. A man was climbing on foot from the creek bottom toward the road where the road made a switchback about a mile's travel ahead of the lead wagon. The man was perfectly visible from John's position, although hidden by rock from the road and by a turn in the creek from the wagon train. He watched longer, saw one other stir of movement below, and a single shaft of gun shine from a promontory looking down from above.

"They's going to be trouble," John said. "Ye got no gun?" He considered giving him one, only the loss of one Navy might serve to unbalance him. "But with only one arm, and that the left, ye couldn't shoot much. But you come along just the same. We got a service to perform, and gun or not you might be useful."

IX

"POWDER AND BALL"

The Widow Cobb drove the parson's wagon as they started at dawn up the Big Hole trail, and by midday he had recovered and felt strong enough to get from his bed and stand braced against the jolt and bang of the wagon and look through the drawstring front aperture at her back.

She saw him and almost fell off the seat from fright. "Git back to bed, oh, mercy on me, I shouldn't've left the poor creetur alone."

"Sister," said the parson, "I feel a mite recovered."

"Oh, glory, glory be! But just think of Mister Cobb, my poor sainted husband, and how he was up one minute with talk about fixing harness, and not three hours later stiff, stark, and turning cold."

He said, complaining a little: "Aren't you pushing a trifle hard for such an old contraption as this?"

"Orders. Royal, Ambrose Stocker. I don't argue. This be the fate of us poor helpless women, just be meek, don't argue with the menfolk, git along the best we can."

High on the rocks, a mile ahead, rode a single, brief glimmer of metal. It could have been Belly River Bob riding scout, but the parson was brought up sharp with suspicion.

"Any hint of Injun trouble?"

She looked surprised. "Why?"

"Nothing, nothing at all, but I'll hold those reins while you go and fetch O'Donnell."

The parson had unusual faith in O'Donnell, considering him the most level-headed man in the lot, and, when he came, he mentioned the gun shine and suggested the advisability of scouting ahead, especially up there half a mile where the road bent out of the blank hillside.

Word quickly ran along the rear half of the wagon train, and after some shouting of questions that portion of it rolled to a halt. In a couple of minutes came Dave Royal, spurring his horse in the narrow space left between the wagons and the bank.

"Gun shine be damned!" he said. "That's our own scout. Come on and roll!"

But the parson was out of his wagon, leaving it to block the way, and was jerking the inside front wheel back and forth.

"Now what the hell?" said Royal. "I thought you were sick."

"This wheel's got to come off."

"Get up there! Get to rolling."

"No!" and the parson faced him like a gaunt, long-necked rooster.

In fury Royal wheeled his horse, trying to slam the parson with the animal's hindquarters. When that failed, in blind fury, although he knew the reaction it would have among the others, he swung a brutal, forearm blow to the side of the old man's neck.

The parson went down, doubled over in the rocks and dirt. Betsy Cobb shouted in dismay and started to jerk her double pistol, but Royal, making another pivot with his horse, smashed it from her hand.

Taking fright, the parson's team lunged, and Betsy had to leave her gun while dragging back on the reins. O'Donnell, unarmed, grabbed up a rock, and Royal, not pausing for an instant, drove his spurs in his horse and rode him down.

Royal came to a stop with his .44 drawn. "I said roll!" he cried in a voice hoarse with rage. "Pick those men up. Keep the wagons together. Roll!"

O'Donnell staggered to his feet, pants torn and thigh bleeding, and still groggy helped the parson into the wagon. The parson suddenly came around and started flapping his arms like a decapitated chicken.

"Git your guns!" he shouted. "There's something afoot. They's some reason they kilt Wood and drove off John. And Rusty. I'll wager he got it, too. Some reason they're set on the Big Hole Pass!"

Royal might have killed him, but O'Donnell had him inside, and the wagons were on the move. At that instant a gun cracked, its far-off report chased by the hand clap sounds of echoes, and, as the wagons slowed and men got their ears up, a high yell came from deep in the creek bottom.

"Injun! Ya-hoo! Injun!"

It was a cry they had feared for the past five weeks. "Don't anyone shoot!" called Royal, riding down the space between wagons and rising mountain with an arm lifted. "I'll parley. If they have us outnumbered, I'll buy 'em off. I'll get your women and kids out safe."

"You mean not even fight for it?" Lafe shouted.

Royal shouted back: "Of course, you don't worry, you don't have any women and kids!"

A wagoner saw someone high on the slope and fired. Royal rode that way, trying to stop him. A volley came from above and below. Shallerbach was on the ground. His wife and the big Nelson boy were dragging him to cover in the wagon.

Some maneuvered their teams producing tangles with other outfits on the narrow road.

One wagon, carried by a bolting team, careened along the edge of the road, jackknifed, and went over with a crash, spilling supplies down the mountain. A flour barrel rolled farthest of all, leaped high, and split itself on a rock with a puff of white. A man crawled clear of the wagon while the horses kicked it to pieces. Most of the wagons had found partial cover against the bank now, and the shooting, after the first flurry, had almost stopped.

Royal rode directly into the open, his beaver hat lifted high, without drawing a shot, but Wally Snite, foolishly attempting to join him, was hit and downed by a long-range bullet. The attackers were then advancing from above and below, and the fight started in earnest.

The parson was down on one knee, an old-time flintlock conversion in his hands, its long barrel poked through a hole in the wagon box, aiming and firing and shouting—"More powder and ball!"—to the Widow Cobb.

"Gimme that gun! Go to bed where you belong."

"Powder and ball! They're closing in." Then he listened. Over the firing and shouting came the faint tone of a voice he recognized. "It's him, it's him!" He hopped to his feet and did a spindly-legged war dance. "Do ye hear it? It's the Comanche! It's Comanche John! We'll tear 'em asunder now, Sister Cobb!"

"Lord help us, you mean Smith *is* Comanche John?"

"He's a ring-tailed ripper from the Rawhide Mountains. And, oh! am I thankful to Leviticus I didn't convert him into laying down his Navies. The trick in this preaching, Sister Cobb, is to convert 'em just so far they ain't varmints and not so far as to make 'em useless."

X

"A RING-TAILED RIPPER"

After a wild descent through the brush of a gully Comanche John reached the creek bottom, Rusty, clinging to the neck of his horse, close on his heels. There they left their horses and climbed on foot. The wagon train was partly halted, and for a moment John thought he might yet reach it before it passed into the range of the ambush, but it started again, so he fired a shot.

He was ready with more, but the one served its purpose, bringing the attack half a mile before its intent. Now renegades were on the move, trying to make their attack on the new position, and John, pushing Rusty to cover, waited for them.

His first volley sent them scattering with one of the half-breeds down, arms outflung, sliding head foremost to a stop among the rock slabs and buck brush. When the others turned to meet his unexpected attack, Rusty lay and drew their fire with his shirt on a branch while John came up from one place and then another, blasting with both Navy Colts.

"Yipee!" he bellowed. "I'm a ring-tailed ripper, I am! I pepper my taters with gunpowder and I eat my meat with the hair on. I kill me a man each day of the year and two on Jeff Davis's birthday jest to be patriotic. I got graveyards named after me all the way from Fraser River to Yuba Gulch, I have for a fact, so give me room because it's my fancy to commence another one on this side hill!"

The scarfaced Indian came down the slope, snaking himself on his belly, and bobbed into view with a rifle to be met and smashed backward by a cross-body shot from John's right-hand Navy. With the scarface gone, the others took to cover, every man for himself, looking only for horses and escape. Higher, about the train, the wagoners had the others in flight. It had become sniping from long range and a plain waste of bullets.

John stood now, and climbed. He found Belly River Bob shot through both legs and groaning: "Don't shoot. I done nothing to you. I'm a wounded man."

John took his guns and flung them ahead of him toward the road as protection against an ambush shot. "Well and good, we'll leave it up to the teamsters what happens to you." He climbed on, muttering: "But we still got the big one left and he's my meat."

"Me?"

He wheeled at the sound of David Royal's voice so close beside him.

The big man had been hiding between two rocks. His Colt was drawn and John would have made a perfect ambush, but he hadn't shot. There was some reason for that.

"Why didn't ye?" asked John, looking into the muzzle of the Colt, chewing, hands dangling below the butts of his holstered Navies.

"Didn't what?"

"Shoot me in the back, of course. Shoot me like ye did Wood."

"I know when I'm beaten." Royal tried to smile but he managed only a wolfish show of teeth. "Beaten all the way around, the girl, the supplies, everything. I'll turn all that over to you. All I want in exchange is your horse. Where is he?"

"Yonder," said John, pointing.

"Take me there."

"Why, sure." He knew that once Royal located the gunpowder he would be a dead man. He glanced beyond Royal and said: "Rusty, whar did ye tie the horses?"

Royal did not flinch. He did not even move his eyes. "Wrong there! Rusty isn't even alive."

"Yes, I am!" said Rusty.

His voice made Royal start around. He could not know that Rusty was unarmed. For an instant the .44 was not aimed, and with the easy shoulder hitch, a sag, and bending of his back, John drew. Royal saw it and shot, but John was in a slightly new position. The .44 slug left a gray mark on a boulder.

Royal tried for a second shot, but his time had run out. The Navies bucked in Comanche's hands, twin reports almost blending with the repeat of the .44, and Royal was spun half around and knocked backward. He kept his feet and started down the mountain. He took ten or twelve steps, preposterous, long, downhill steps, before he lost balance and fell face first in a tangle of juniper. There he lay very still, with the mountain breeze waving a lock of his light brown hair.

"Finished," John said, blowing smoke from the barrels of his guns. "No, Rusty, don't go near the horses. There's renegades yonder. The gunpowder will come when I whistle, and your horse will follow. Poor time to get killed now when there'll be supper coming up. By grab, come to think of it, I forgot to eat in a day or two."

With difficulty the wagons were turned in the narrow trail,

and now they rolled back toward the forks. Rusty, with his head bandaged and his broken arm in splints and a sling, sat beside Lela in the high seat of her wagon, their shoulders touching, neither of them speaking, their happiness too complete.

The parson in his wagon kept craning around at each bend, trying to glimpse them, saying: "Yep, yep! I *will* have a marriage to perform."

In the Shallerbach wagon, Belly River Bob lay bandaged, unable to use his legs, and Ambrose Stocker came around to John, almost doffing his hat and bowing for reverence.

"John," he said, "what do you think we should do with that scoundrel? Personally I'm for hanging."

"No-o," John said, pondering, aiming at a bit of whitish porphyry by the road, tobacco-juicing it fair center, "I ain't for hanging on a wagon train. It never seemed proper to me. I say save that scoundrel for Hell Gate. They got a judge there, and a miner's jury. Let them hang him. It'll liven things up, and they'll appreciate it. Git ye off on the right foot."

Walking, moving from one wagon to the other, the Widow Cobb was saying: "Well, I never! Never in all my days have I seen the equal of that parson of ours. A miracle, that's what it was. Last night, you can take my word for it, he had turned blue. Yes, blue all over. The heartbeat was gone and there was no breath in him. Well, I 'low, I'd've laid him out if I had had his clothes ironed. And now look at him! Gunfighting with a rifle and traveling on his own two pins. I say let them that scoff at miracles just see what I beholden today."

Then each time she would locate John and try to get close to him, but John always had something to do at a far end of the train.

Camped at the old place by the forks, John was not there

for supper. At midnight he crept in the parson's wagon and started rummaging for cold biscuits.

"What's the matter with you?" the parson asked, rousing in bed, knowing in the dark who it was. "No hangman is looking for you now."

"I'm not coming near this train again," said John through biscuits. "I'm camping a safe three miles ahead. That widda is enamored o' me. She buried one husband I know about, and. . . ."

"Why, John. She wouldn't kill ye off. Be a fine wife. . . ."

"Waal, maybe, but it seems to me she has a great fancy for funerals. I watched her, Parson, and I don't like the way she looks at me, like she was measuring me off. And do you know what she said to me one time? She said . . . 'Brother John, do you own a black serge suit?' No, sir . . . once this creaky outfit gits to Hell Gate, ye'll see me no more. It'll be a Blackfeet gal for me."

Stuffing his pockets with biscuits, John dropped from the rear of the wagon, and the parson, propped on his elbows, listening, could hear the *clip-clop* of the gunpowder's hoofs, and John's monotonous voice bumped from him as he rode away:

Comanche John rode to I-de-ho
In the year of 'Sixty-Two.
Oh! Listen to my storee,
I'll tell ye what he do. . . .

The Fastest Gun Thar Be

I

"EL DORADO BOUND"

The stagecoach driver was a tall, loose, red-mustached man much fortified by three big slugs from the stationkeeper's bottle. He climbed to the seat of the Concord and shouted: "Git aboard or git left behind! It's ho! for the gold fields of Shauvegan, El Dorado, and Chinee Gulch, and I'm half an hour late already!"

In response, ten passengers crowded inside and an eleventh, a middling broad, black-whiskered man, maneuvered himself and his brace of Navy Colt pistols to the hurricane where he got placed with his jackboots on the seat between the shotgun guard and the driver. Gee-hawing the lines that ran far out across the backs of his six-horse team, the driver shouted—"Let 'em rumble!"—at which the half-breed lad holding the leaders let go and dived for his life. "Ya-how!" shouted the driver, standing and swinging his long lash, and the horses, freshly hitched for the pull up Moosehorn Pass, almost jumped out of their hides and were off at a run with the coach wildly careening behind them. Never were more than three of the coach's wheels on earth at once, and at times not any, but still the whooping driver urged them on; the whiskered man and the guard held tightly, and the scene inside the coach was one of scrambled and cursing humanity.

After half a mile, with some of the vinegar burned from his

team, the driver eased back, handling each horse just so with his double handfuls of ribbons until they were all pulling right and the coach rocked along behind them as easily as a hammock.

They had entered a deep gulch with forested mountains rising to bald pinnacles on each side. There were evening shadows, an evening chill sharpened by the fragrance of pine, and the black-whiskered man shivered and tied the fastenings of his buckskin jacket.

"That Bannack City highlife was nigh the finish of me," he said. "Regular meals, sleeping in a bed . . . I tell ye, it softens a man up. All very well when you're young, but when ye git to crowding forty, *no*. Especially when you're crowding it the wrong way." He hitched his Navy Colts to more comfortable positions, aimed a spurt of tobacco juice at some rocks projecting from one side of the road, and asked: "At what o'clock will ye rise the Chinee Diggings?"

"It'll be black as a gambler's heart when we make the top of the pass, and the Redwillow and Sulphurwater are both high. Last trip I was half an hour at Sulphurwater hunting a crossing. I'd say we'd hove the diggings by midnight. That's the diggings, though. You're bound for New Boston. New Boston is five, six mile farther along."

The coach splashed across a shallow stream and started upgrade on a road dug from the loose sand rock of the mountain. Making himself comfortable with one boot on the break, the driver rolled his eye at the shotgun guard and added: "Yep, midnight, if we don't meet up with road agents."

The guard, heavy-set and truculent, said: "This is an incoming coach. Who the hell would be crazy enough to rob an incoming one?"

"Did at the Yallerstone this spring. Banks in the country now. Banks bring in greenbacks. And I hear that Comanche

John has moved in here from Idaho."

The guard knew he was being needled, but he could not help bristling back: "I hope that braggart does try to rob my outfit sometime. I only hope so." He whacked the Eight-Gauge shotgun between his knees. "Because, if he does, I'll hit him with a quarter pound of Number Two buck and turn him so the hair side's in."

The black-whiskered man said: "Coman-che? Ye mean he's an Injun?"

"No Injun. Pike County white man, if you can call Missourians white. Dirty bushwhacking, killing, robbing, woolly wolf!"

The driver said: "Robs from the rich and gives to the poor."

"Hah!"

Whereupon the driver got his chew of tobacco off to one side and lifted his voice in song:

> There's forty dozen highwaymen
> 'Twixt Denver and the sea,
> But I sing of old Comanche John
> The fastest gun thar be.
> He robs the bank, he robs the stage,
> He robs the Union mail,
> And he's left his private graveyards
> All along the Bannack Trail.

The black-whiskered man said: "That was *purty*. Can't believe a man could be so bad and have such a song written about him. Would ye mind singing some more?"

The guard shouted: "No, don't sing any more! That damn' song'll end by driving me crazy. Anyhow, it don't make no never mind because the Comanche is dead. I heered he was hung by the vigilantes over in I-de-ho City."

"That's what I heered, too!" said the black-whiskered one. "He's low in his grave so nobody needs to be looking for him, and that's a relief. That *is* a relief!" To prove that he blew his breath and removed his black slouch hat to wipe away some imaginary perspiration. "But I would like to hear some more of that song."

> Co-man-che rode to Yallerjack
> On the twelfth day of July,
> With chawin' tobacco in his mouth
> And killin' in his eye,
> Upon his head an old slouch hat
> And boots above the knee,
> A faster shootin' highwayman
> You seldom ever see.
> Now Co-man-che had a pardner
> By the name of Whiskey Ike,
> And the only motto that they had
> Was share and share alike.
> They robbed the coach at Uniontown
> They robbed the. . . .

"Quit it, quit that caterwauling!" cried the guard. "I got to look and listen both on this job."

The driver still ruminated the song under his breath for a while, then he said to the black-whiskered man: "I don't want to be misunderstood, but that description of the Comanche does cut you right down the middle."

"I'm just a poor pilgrim on the trail of life. Brown's the handle. John Brown, and no relation to that varmint they hung at Harper's Ferry. Besides, as ye say, the Comanche is low in his grave at I-de-ho City. . . ."

"They hung him in Yankee Flats and in Placerville, too. By grab, I never see a man that was hung so often as that Comanche John." He rolled an eye on the jittery guard. "How about you, McCabe?"

"He tries to rob my coach they won't need to hang him."

Darkness settled gradually throughout the two hour pull to the crest. Topping it, they could see dimly, by a glow from the west, a vast timber and mountain country, the snowy summits of the Gold Creek Range to the northeast, and straight away, some miles below, a tiny twinkle of lights.

"New Boston?" asked the whiskered man.

"No. New Boston is hid in the gulch. That's the Irish Bar, a bench placer. Torchlight, work night and day. Git the gold out fast and turn the country back to the Injuns, that's the ticket!"

The coach entered timber and started down a steep drop with the brakes rubbing. It was very dark there. The driver had a hard time keeping his leaders moving fast enough, while the swing team, more than willing now that the pull was over, threatened to tangle the harness. There was a sharp turn, and the leaders suddenly came to a stop with the other horses all crowding them.

The driver cursed fluently, managing the lines with one hand and putting his weight on the brake with the other. The shotgun guard, on his feet, peered ahead, and the whiskered man, sensing danger, moved crab-like back across the hurricane with a thought of escaping over the side, but a voice, high-pitched and obviously disguised, came from the blackness of the mountain bank close beside them: "Hands up!"

The guard, after freezing for half a second, started around with the shotgun. There was a flash of powder, the deafening crash of a gun exploding at close range, and he went down, stomach across the seat, knees on the footrest.

Frightened, the horses tried to bolt. There was a log from the bank across the road that turned the lead team. The driver gee-hawed and cursed and got the horses stopped without going off the road where the coach would surely have capsized on the steep side of the mountain.

"The guard, he's going to fall," said the black-whiskered man, hands raised, the bandit covering him. "You better let me grab him."

"All right, but you reach for your guns, I'll blast your innards clear to Hangtown."

The guard was wounded through the chest and bleeding rather badly from the region of his right armpit. The black-whiskered man managed to drag his 180 pounds up the seat to the hurricane where he rolled him face down and held him.

A man, disguising his voice with a French accent, came alongside calling to the passengers: "Stay een-side. Firs' man out I keel. Firs' man try potshot I reedle whole coach weeth buckshot."

There were others in movement, dim shapes in the darkness marked by the shine of pistols and shotguns. A light appeared. It was a tin-can lantern with air vents top and bottom and a door that opened to give light or closed to conceal it as the occasion demanded.

The man carrying it issued a few low orders. Obviously he was the leader, and the black-whiskered one watched him on that account. He wore a blanket to hide his clothes; a handkerchief was pinned to the brim of his hat. All of them wore blankets and masks. After a brief conference the leader stepped back and stood very erect, watching three of the others pull mail sacks from the boot.

"Cut 'em open!" he said in a low voice, and they slit the sacks one after another with their Bowies and strewed letters and parcels over the ground beneath the lantern light. It was

86

apparent they were looking for one bit of mail in particular, and finally it turned up in the form of a large, starched linen envelope with dabs of wax around the flap.

"That's him," said one of the men indicating the name with his thumb.

"Better open it," said the leader.

The man tried but the stiffened linen was very tough. He made with the Bowie, but the leader checked him, saying— "Later."—and took the letter and put it away inside his blanket, and inside his shirt, too.

The black-whiskered man, leaning over the side of the coach, muttered: "By grab, if that didn't look like the parson's name." That first big letter was the same, he was sure of that, and that next big one was a fishhook, and the next was a loop-ended ramrod, and that could add up to be the Reverend Jeremiah Parker.

"How about the strongbox?" one of the men asked. "What a hell of a gang, take paper and leave the strongbox."

So they dumped it off and spent some time with a prospector's pick chopping the lock off.

"Greenbacks?" one asked as its contents were pawed.

"No, not a damn' thing. Hold on, here's some watches. By doggies, I'm not leaving a box of fifty dollar watches."

"Yes, flash one and end on a hang rope. Let's move!"

The lantern went out. There was low talk back and forth. Someone was leading saddle horses down the steep bank to the road. Men were leaving, but still guns were there, watchful for trouble. Then those left, there was a *clatter* of departing hoofs, and everybody in the coach commenced shouting at once.

"It's the Crow Rock gang," one of them said. And another: "The Crow Rock nothing, they don't get this far from Idaho, that was Dutch Hymie and Little Bob." The driver quieted them all: "No, it warn't the Crow Rock gang and it warn't Dutch and Bob, neither. What do you back-Easterners know about hold-up men, anyhow? I tell you, I been robbed by 'em all. You see that one yonder in the black hat? The way he stood there, spread-legged! And the way he held those Navies! Tell you there's only one man in all the West holds his Navies like that, and that's the rippingest, rearingest, shootingest ya-hoo that ever come up the long trail from Californy. Yes, gents, he was nobody else than the one and only Comanche John!"

II

"RAISED ON CATFISH
AND CORN LIKKER"

They rolled down the dark, winding road with the guard bandaged and resting easily on top of the coach, the whiskered man tending him, and the driver singing with fine spirit:

> Oh, halter up your pony
> And listen unto me,
> Whilst I sing of old Comanche John
> The fastest gun thar be.
> He was born back in Missouri,
> 'Twas in the County Pike,
> And whenever he draws his twin Navies
> 'Tis share and share alike.
> He had a pal named Jimmy Dale
> And one called Dirty Bob . . .

"Make him quit it," whispered the guard, trying to struggle up while the whiskered man restrained him. "That bushwhacking Comanche, if I. . . ."

"Waren't the Comanche, I'll *guarantee* ye it waren't the Comanche!" And added to himself: *Ought to know, because I'm the Comanche myself!*

They reached the stage station at Sulphurwater where the shotgun guard was put to bed. There Comanche John left the coach, purchased from the stationkeeper a fair-looking bay horse and a Pennsylvania saddle, paying over a heavy poke of Bannack gold dust without haggling over the outrageous price, and, as the stage rolled on, he was also on his way, at a trot and gallop through the night, following a cut-across toward the mining camp of New Boston.

The bandits, he reasoned, were local or they would not have been so carefully masked; they were not ordinary robbers, either, or the strongbox would not have been an afterthought, nor would the passengers have gone untouched.

"By grab, I wish I could read," he muttered, riding up a timbered gulch, holding wire-hard pine branches away from his face. That envelope—he was certain it had been addressed to the Reverend Jeremiah Parker, the same reverend that had plucked him from the black gulch of sin more than a twelve-month ago.

Half an hour of hard riding put him at the crest of a ridge. There he paused to let his horse breathe and had a look around. New Boston was yonder, but the gulch poked deep into the hills, and he had a hunch they had gone that way. For men on horseback it would be shorter and easier, and it was always a good idea for a highwayman to be in camp looking innocent when the coach arrived.

Pushing hard again, he rode cut-across toward the diggings. It was downhill for a mile. He crossed a tiny creek roily-yellow from placer mining farther up, then he wound through pine-covered hills toward a saddle in a ridge, the only easy passage available for several miles.

He reined in. They would surely come this way. He freshened his chew. He sang a bit of that pesky Comanche John song that the muleskinners had made up about him—all eighty-nine verses of it about him. He got one jackboot hooked around the saddle horn for comfort and looked long across the country. It was bright with black shadows under the moon, and no movement anywhere.

He was about to ride on when the note of a man's voice touched his ear, a voice very distant but still distinct through the night's clearness, and looking back and across the saddle, half a mile away, he saw the moving shapes of horsemen, eight or nine of them—or perhaps even ten, he could not be sure.

He rode, keeping among the pines, staying just so far ahead as the moon rose slowly through clouds like curdled milk, and midnight approached. The riders found a trail and turned from sight into a gulch. In the distance he could see a line of torches—a placer mine. This, he decided, was Shauvegan Gulch or the Chinee Diggings, either of which would lead to New Boston.

He made his decision then and spurred to a gallop, reaching the gulch ahead of them. He found a well-traveled trail and gambled on them taking it. He waited among pines, heard the *click-clack* of hoofs, a voice or two. He waited.

A horseman rode into sight, then another. No masks or blankets now. Neither, he thought, was the leader, although he could not be sure. He let them pass. They were hidden by timber down the trail with their companions not yet in sight. He spoke to his horse, nudged him with the heel of one jackboot, and rode out, falling in behind them.

He maintained a slow jog, letting the next riders overtake him.

"That you, Hoss?" a voice said. "How the tarnation . . . I thought you was behint me."

Instead of answering, John lifted a hand in response and let the man come up to him. He was tall and slouched with hair that fell to his shoulders and a stringy, blond mustache. He was scarcely a long reach away when he suddenly realized that this was not "Hoss"—that, indeed, it was not even one of his associates. He reined up and started for the Navy at his hip, but with a sag of his right shoulder Comanche John had already drawn, and the gun was cocked and aimed.

"No, don't lift your hands. Just keep riding. That's it, right beside me. Now, whar's the envelope?"

"I don't have it."

No, he wasn't the leader. He didn't have the leader's voice, and he didn't have his erect manner, either.

Two others were coming. "What's the trouble, Huck?" one of them asked, and he *was* the leader.

He came at a trot still not realizing that anything was amiss until he caught the shine of light on the drawn Navy.

The man's response was sudden. He spurred, reined sharply around, and went for his right-hand gun. His companion coming up behind him got in his way. A horse reared, a man was dumped to the ground, a horse bolted, crashing through brush toward the creek.

Darkness and mêlée made Comanche John momentarily lose track of things. Then he saw the leader with his gun out, and, spurring forward, he clubbed the man from his saddle.

He holstered his Navy, swung to the ground, held his lunging horse with one hand and ripped the man's shirt open with the other, and there was the envelope, bent the shape of his chest, warm from contact with his body. He twisted it into a roll, thrust it inside his belt, and remounted as the leader, coming to, started getting to his feet.

John, fighting his frightened horse, made a flash appraisal. Down the gulch he would have to ride through open moonlight. In the other direction men bore down on him, but it was dark, and darkness suited his mood. He spoke to the horse—

"Git, dang ye!"—and spurred.

"That's him!" a man was braying. "That's him right among you!"

He bent low as a gun exploded with flame bursting in his face. He could feel the wind whip of passing lead. One ear was deaf and ringing. He bumped another horseman. He was in the open. Guns exploded behind him, and he answered, twisted about in the saddle.

A man grunted, cursed, and cried: "Damn you, Step-And-A-Half, don't ride me down!"

There was moonlight, a stretch of open trail. He did not enter it. He pulled in hard almost making his horse fall. The creek, through willow brush, murmured below. Hanging to the neck of his horse, hat over his face, he plunged through the tangle of bushes and found himself deep in the creek.

The horse struggled to carry him. There was sand and a deep hole by some old logs. Water flowed coldly through a rent in one boot, the same boot he'd had repaired in Bannack. He cursed the shoemaker and kept going with a steep bank on both sides and bushes bowering above.

Men were above him, to the left. He could hear them, sometimes no more than long-spitting distance away, but the brush and their own noise saved him. There was a low place on the other bank. He turned his horse and climbed it, rode across a gravel bar, down through a swamp of an old beaver dam, a place fragrant of horse mint where mosquitoes rose in shadowy clouds so he had to beat them from his hands and face.

He reached some flats. It was easy going. He maintained a steady trot. Sound of pursuit had vanished. There was a blessed night quiet and the envelope making a satisfying bulge in his belt. Ahead half a mile burned the pitch torches of a placer mine—a deep cut, a bank of gray-white gravel, a head box, some sluices on high piles, a look-out's shanty, men standing by their wheelbarrows still looking, wondering what the shooting had been.

"I do hope this be the parson's envelope," he muttered. "I do wonder what the tarnation would be in it that'd cause 'em to mighty near pass up a strongbox to git to it!"

III

"NOT THE MARRYING KIND"

The road led him on a winding course among the cuts and gravel heaps of placer mines to New Boston where the coach had just rolled in. He took a back street among shanties, tents, and dugouts, beneath a flume that dripped on him, through a ramshackle Chinatown with its peculiar smells and its banners hanging over the street.

He rode warily, his black slouch hat down over his eyes, his Navies with their butts out in easy reach, but he met no one, and finally he reached his destination—the rear door of a long log structure with a makeshift steeple.

He opened the door and spoke into the darkness: "Parson! Parson, be ye thar? It's Comanche John."

"John, John!" the parson cried, startled from sleep. "Here, let me feel of you." He came barefoot, groping, and felt him up and down. "Yes, it *is*. Oh, blessed day! I read in the Salt Lake paper that they'd hung ye dead down in Idaho City."

"Yes, and tomorrow ye'll hear that I robbed the New Boston coach."

"John, ye didn't! Ye haven't gone back to your old ways of wretchedness!"

"Don't worry about me, Parson. I ain't no fair-weather

Christian. When I hit the sawdust trail, I hit her hard. So help me, I haven't tooken a single coach except maybe one with some Union gov'ment payroll, and I wouldn't have touched that only for the war, and I seen it as my patriotic duty to the Confederacy. But I did get something off that coach tonight. This envelope, and it war addressed to you. Leastwise thar be a capital fishhook and a capital loop-end, ramrod-like, I seen often enough at the for'ard ends of Jeremiah Parker."

The parson blew a pitch-pine twig to flame and carried it to a candle. He was gaunt and old. His legs which protruded from his nightshirt were all tendons and bone. Gray hair fell to his shoulders. He had a long neck, a pointed Adam's apple, a sharp, high nose, and a pair of protruding eyeballs. "Like a plucked buzzard," as John had remarked in his more unflattering moments.

"Letter for me?" The parson took it. "From Saint Joe. The Honorable Eborum Black. Why, that's the lawyer. I know what this be. This is the gov'ment deed to our end of White Pine Valley."

He broke the seals and tore the envelope flap loose, taking out a stiff, folded square of parchment ornately inscribed by hand, sealed with gold and wax. "Why, this be the original grant made to the Western Fur Company. See thar . . . Eighteen Forty-Six! And look at whose name's signed . . . James J. Polk, President of the United States!"

"So that's it!" said John spitting his satisfaction at the ash hopper. "So that's why they was after the coach. That's a mighty valuable paper, Parson. If you and them Kansas pilgrims value your homes, I'd hide that some place. I'd hide it good!"

"It ain't for me to hide. It's for Ambrose Stocker to hide, and we'd better take it to him tonight."

Stocker was the leader of a group of emigrants that Comanche John had guided over from the Snake River side last autumn. This valley of theirs, the White Pine, into which flowed Chinee, Shauvegan, and El Dorado gulches had been purchased from the executors of the old Western Fur Company at bankruptcy proceedings in St. Louis before they set out. That, of course, had been the parson's doing. The parson was a great one for bringing in wagon trains of flat-broke farmers and plowing up the West establishing homes and all that, and John humored him even though he knew nothing would come of it, that late or soon they'd all move out and turn the country back to the Indians.

When this group arrived before snow the fall before, the nearest settlements were at Hell Gate and Hangtown, but scarcely had they made camp when rich gravel was struck in Chinee Gulch, and then in Shauvegan and El Dorado, starting a stampede so that within a matter of weeks the gulches were staked from the White Pine to headwaters. Miners sunk a few deep prospect holes in the White Pine, too, but an abundance of water prevented any of them reaching bedrock.

The emigrants, of course, joined the rush, men and women both, but with indifferent success. Gold may be "where you find it", but you generally find it distributed with regard to certain natural laws that the California men understand and the emigrants didn't. Of them all, only O'Donnell really "struck the color", and, although his bench claim on Shauvegan had good values, the pay streak was wandering, huge boulders had to be moved to reach it, and aside from spring and early summer, when a snow freshet from a side gully was running, he had no water for his sluice. Gold mining is not always what it's cracked up to be.

Putting his clothes on, the parson said: "You better come

yonder with me. There's a woman got a desire to see you."

"The Widder Cobb? I don't know, Parson. I don't know about that. She tried to rope and hog-tie me. She got matrimony on her mind."

But John was a trifle chary of sending him alone with the government grant—they knew it was addressed to the parson and they might be waiting. No one was, though, and they left camp without incident, crossed some little barren hills, and dropped down on the grass-deep bottoms of the White Pine.

The valley, aside from its mosquitoes, was about all a homemaker could wish for. There was pasture to a cow's belly, water in abundance for irrigation, and high ground for oats, spuds, and corn. There were even buildings ready-made—the old stockade, sheds, blockhouses, and trade house of the fur company built twenty years before and abandoned after the collapse of the fur market.

John said: "They should turn a fancy dollar on their crop what with gold flowing like water and spuds selling at two bits a pound."

"That's what I'm skeered of," said the parson. "Too much money's worse'n not enough. A heap worse."

"That all depends on the indy-vigil," said John judiciously. "Now, me, when I cut the big pay streak, I'll be mighty wise. Git me a Blackfeet gal, I will. Build me a snug shanty for winter and a teepee for summer. Oh, o' course, I'll buy me some fancy trappings, and a red dress for my squaw, but the rest of my money I'll salt away, invest it in something that'll pay a steady interest like good, safe Confederate bonds."

They rode through the gate of the stockade and up to the old trade house where the parson stuck his head in the door and called: "Stocker, wake up! I'm the parson and I got something for ye!"

Stocker, a huge man built on the lines of a bull buffalo, came in carrying a candle in one hand, pulling his plow-line suspenders over his shoulders, looking ill-tempered and bleary. He saw John and asked: "You on the jump again? By grannies, we're not having trouble with the law here and we don't figure to have."

"After I saved your hides and your outfits back on the pass," said John, "thanks fest the welcome."

"Well, I ain't ungrateful. Only a body has to think of such things."

"If you're worried about the law, I'll tell ye something. Legally I'm not here at all. Legally, I'm in I-de-ho, and I got me a affy-david of the death certificate to prove it."

Stocker took the grant and looked at it. Other men came in—Lafe Crocker, Dilworth, Shallerbach, and sneaking around in the rear was weasel-faced Wally Snite.

"You don't need to hide thar, Snite," John said. "Come along in. I already kilt my man for the day."

John could not endure the sight of the sodbusters and left to visit the Widow Cobb who had her cap perched to marry him, a risk John was willing to run, in order to fill himself with her cornmeal fritters, cob syrup, and homemade butter, the finest in all the West. He left her doing dishes and sneaked away to saddle his horse.

The parson, finding him, said: "You can't leave already. We just. . . ."

"I can and I am. That widda woman is enamored o' me, and I doubt I'd fit in double harness. Probably be a plow on the other end of it. No, I'm a ring-tailed ripper from the Raw-hide Mountains, like the poet said. I sleep with my boots on and I still got cockleburs in my hair I picked up in Coloraydo. I have for a fact, and all that don't make me the marrying kind."

IV

"SHOOTIN' ACQUAINTANCES"

He slept in the open, a cushion of spruce boughs under him, his saddle blanket over his shoulders, awakening at hour intervals to shiver away the mountain cold. In the morning he shot a blue grouse and roasted it on a prop stick, eating half and saving the other half for dinner. That night he was at French Pete's ranch on the Redwillow where he had left his gunpowder roan pony at pasture the winter before.

The pony was wild and hard to catch, sleek from the rich grass that grew in the bottoms, but he grew tractable once he had John's familiar weight on his back and John's familiar voice in his ear. Mounted on the gunpowder and leading the bay, he rode to Silversides, a five-shanty mining camp to the north of the Hell Gate freight road. There, giving an ear to rumors of a rich showing on Hellroaring Creek, he turned farther north, entering a trackless wilderness of mountain and forest, living for three days on the trout he slapped in the grizzly fashion from stream riffles, at last coming on Hellroaring where eight bearded men were shacked up in two side-gulch dugouts, pitting the flanks of the watercourse with prospect holes.

John staked gravel and worked almost an entire day, but

his claim did not show the color. He commenced working his way upstream, panning the benches and side gullies, his eye out for rusty quartz outcroppings that might indicate the mother lode.

He gave up and crossed to the east, working his way toward the diggings at Montana City, but great ridges of mountains lay between, and, after days of toil up one cañon after another, he found no landmark, near or distant, that was familiar. He saw smoke and headed toward it. He found a village of Flathead Indians. He rested for a day, filled himself with venison and camas stew, got directions, and rode to the camp of Irish Bar, a mile off Blackfoot River.

He bucked a faro game. Loser, he sold his extra horse and part of his outfit, and he lost that. He had been cold-decked. He brooded about it. Late at night, the place almost empty, candles burning low, the dealer off at the bar for a whiskey, John got up from the chair where he pretended to be asleep, drew his Navies, and requested assistance of the look-out and casekeeper in carrying the bank box of gold outside. He did it so quietly that none of the half dozen others in the place even glanced around.

Outside, dawn was glowing through the spruce trees, but it was quite dark in the rubbish-littered area behind the saloon.

"Don't try anything, boys," John said, "because I got eyes like a lynx brought up in a coal mine, and, if I had to shoot one of ye, t'other would be saddled with the task of carrying this treasure by his lonesome and that ain't my idea of equity."

He rode south, following no trail. It was fine to be a man of wealth again, and fine to feel the solid satisfaction of a deed well done. He rested at a prospector's shanty and rode on, leaving the mountains, crossing sage-covered hills to Montana City.

The camp was scattered for miles, a cluster of houses here and a cluster there separated by acres of washed gravel that turned white in the sun. He sat in the shadowy depths of the camp's largest saloon and gave ear to the talk around him, but the news of his Irish Bar robbery had not preceded him. Montana City cared not one damn for anything except Montana City gold, and that was how it should be, each camp minding its own business and not out with ropes meddling in somebody else's road agents. He had a bath. He had a haircut and beard trim at a lady barber's. He emerged brushed and perfumed. He bought a new shirt, a white linen one. He drank fancy wine. He did the polka with a beautiful, broad brunette in the Golden Slipper dance hall. There was a four-room hotel where he put up at $12 a night, but the softness of the bed troubled him, so he arose and slept rolled in a blanket by the creek. Next morning, emerging from a restaurant with a toothpick in his teeth and his stomach filled with side meat, Mormon eggs, and chopped fried potatoes, he heard the *thum-tumming* of a banjo and a familiar voice raised defiantly in song:

> **Comanche John rode to Singleshot**
> **With a pal named Jimmy Dale.**
> **And just for some excitement**
> **They robbed the northern mail.**
> **Now Jimmy's six foot underground**
> **And much he rues the day,**
> **Whilst Comanche rides the long cou-lée**
> **Tryin' to git away.**

John whacked the legs of his homespuns and said: "Why, damn me, it's White Eyes!"

White Eyes was roosted on a barrel beneath the pole

awning of the stage station, a tall man turning gray, looking out with milky, sightless eyes. He stopped singing and reached out with the banjo in the hope someone would drop gold in it, but no one was close.

"Hold it," said John, slouching up, and dropped in a two ounce nugget. "Thar, how ye like *that* metal?"

Sound of John's voice made White Eyes move as though his barrel had caught fire. "Yipee," he said, restraining his voice. "It's the old Comanche himself! They said ye wouldn't dare stay in Montana once they got the print shop posters up, but I said . . . 'You wait and you see, the Comanche will come and he'll go and he'll leave dead Yankees and robbed coaches behint him each turn of the way!' "

"I settled down a mite, White Eyes. Me for the quiet life. I staked me some gulch gravel on Hellroaring, worked it with my own hands, toiled from sunup to sundown, and now I got me a considerable weight of metal, only I didn't exactly git it thar."

"*You* settled down? I'll never see that day. Nor you, neither." Then he whispered: "I got a message for ye."

"For me? How'd they know I'd come to Montana City when I didn't know it myself?"

"Reckon they knew you'd always find your old friend, White Eyes. We drawn to each other, John. We. . . ."

"Message from who?"

"That sky pilot parson back in New Boston. He says for ye to come back. I don't know what he means by it, but he says they haven't heered the last of that robbery at Moosehorn. Did ye rob a coach at Moosehorn Pass, John? Did ye? It'd make a fine verse for your song. . . ."

"Waal, no, I didn't, but I robbed the boys that robbed the coach at Moosehorn, how'd that be?"

He saddled and rode, and again it was night, and again he

spoke to the parson through the back door of his mission.

"Thank heaven ye came," said the parson. "I need ye, John. Need ye bad."

"Those damn' farmers, ain't it? By grab, don't you ever mix me up with a bunch of punkin-rollers again. How you ever expect me to make my fortune so I can ree-tire and take life easy like I deserve? What they done now? I suppose they lost that gov'ment grant. Got it stole from 'em."

"It's gone," moaned the parson deep in misery. "Not stole, thank the Lord for that. Burned up in a fire. But *they* don't know it's burned up, so. . . ."

"Who don't?"

"Those claim-jumpers . . . Huckven, Overfelt, Hoss Noon. Do you know what they did, John? Come in by the dark of night and put up their claim markers all over the best parts of the White Pine. Well, Stocker and the boys run 'em off, and now they have the law working. That drunken Judge Harrison . . . his variety of law."

"This happened *before* ye lost the grant?"

"After. Oh, if we *had* it, it'd be different. The law'd be on our side then. Of course, we were there *first*. Even Judge. . . ."

"But what if *they* show up with the grant? What then?"

"It was burned."

"Maybe it was," John muttered. "But then maybe, just *maybe*. . . ."

"John, I don't know what to do. I'm gittin' near the end of my days. I can feel the cold of the grave settling in my bones. I'm weary and bowed with care."

"You're tough as bull jerky," said John with no sympathy.

"No, I ain't, the twilight of my days are here, and I got only one last wish . . . to see those farmers snug and safe in their homes, to see the broad valley of the White Pine green and yaller with their crops. I saved your neck from the hang rope, John. I saved it for a purpose, because I figured there was more good in ye than evil, and this is your chance to prove I was right. This'll prove I was right and those vigilantes was wrong. So save it for me, John. Save the White Pine!"

"I'll do it!" said John. "I'll save these punkin-rollers their homes and farms if I have to beat their heads with my Navy guns and marry Sister Cobb . . . I'll do it!"

Comanche John slept at the mission, and come morning he moseyed out on the street. No one recognized him; he saw himself on no reward posters. He sat in plain sight in a willow-weave chair on the porch of the new Territorial Hotel, chewed and spit across the plank walk, and watched a steady press of men and freight outfits along the street without seeing a single person he ever remembered seeing before. The big rush now was up the Missouri by steamboat to Fort Benton, and down on the new freight road through Last Chance and Montana City, and, while only a twelve-month ago the California men were in a majority, now they were mostly busted farmers, Army deserters, and draft dodgers, the untanned, untried flotsam of the East.

Leaving town with the parson, he said: "If I ever seen a conclave of Abolitionists, this camp of New Boston is it. I 'low, if I cut loose with my Navies, I'd empty this camp in five minutes."

"There's *some* you wouldn't empty the town of, and I mean Clip Overfelt, and Hoss Noon, and Missou, and Huckven and Billy Step-And-A-Half. They were run out of Californy, and run out of Snake River, and run off from Bannack. . . ."

"And now they're staking your farm land!"

"The very ones!"

Hoss, John was thinking. He remembered someone being

called Hoss that night of the hold-up. And he seemed to recall one being called Step-And-A-Half, too. He said: "How about a tall, limber one with sort of a loose jaw and a yaller mustache like so?"

"That's Huckven. Government wants him for murdering Injuns down on the Paiute preserve, or so I'm told. You acquainted with him?"

"I had a shootin' acquaintance. I had a shootin' acquaintance with all of 'em, but it war dark. I doubt I'll be known."

It didn't seem reasonable, their staking the bottoms. Any gold there would be deep under thirty or forty feet of overburden, and mining it would be *work,* and work never appealed to men of their stamp. He said as much, and the parson answered.

"They can't mine the White Pine by drifting or any other way. Too much water. Sink a hole anywhere, you have a well in thirty feet. And it's too flat for hydraulics. That's what puzzles me. Why stake the bottoms when there's no chance of mining it?"

"They could scoop and skid with a drag bucket and one of those high washers like I seen in Californy. They're the latest wrinkle, Parson. Backfill the tails into the excavation and use the same water over and over. But who'd know about *that* fancy system in this camp? Not that dirty Huckven. I'll wager they got a man behind 'em with brains. By grab, Parson, it *is* lucky ye sent for me!"

Lafe Crocker sat in a rocking chair outside the stockade with a Jager rifle beside him, keeping watch.

Crocker said no, there had been no trouble, not a sign of trouble. "We figure they'll try it the legal way first," he said. "They delivered a paper just yesterday signed by Judge Harrison."

The parson led John to the remains of a burned block-house. "It was hid there. Hid in a can between the logs on the second floor. Couldn't help but be burned."

John raked the ashes and found the can crushed flat by fallen timbers that later burned. He got the can open. There was no parchment, of course. Heat would have consumed it. But there should have been ashes and at least some remnants of the heavy gold seal that had been affixed to it, and the can was empty of anything.

"It was stole," John said. "Then the man that stole it set the fire so your boys wouldn't know it was stole. All of a sudden they'll get ye into court and flash it on ye, and that grant wasn't made over to anybody. Whoever owns the grant owns the land. So keep 'em off. Fight 'em off. Meantime, I got an idee to git it back."

"What you aim to do?"

"Jine 'em. Yep, Parson, come tomorrow Huckven, Overfelt, and Hoss Noon will have a new associate."

V

"A CALIFORNIA MAN"

Comanche John sat with his chair tilted against the rear wall of the saloon, his black slouch hat over his eyes, moving only when he aimed tobacco juice at the sawdust box that served as a spittoon. It was late afternoon, still light outside, but here in the low, long, almost windowless saloon building half a dozen lamps were on. A faro game moved listlessly. Four miners and a down-at-the-heel gambler in greenish serge and a Louisiana planter's hat .played poker. At the bar several men were drinking, and one of them was whooping and beating the bar with his fist in the delight of telling his exploits among the squaws of the Palouse tribe over in Walla Walla country. That noisy one was Missou, one of the gang who had been in on the robbery at Moosehorn.

Now two other members of the gang came in. One John recognized as Clip Overfelt, the leader, and the other was Billy Step-And-A-Half, a rusty-complexioned man of twenty-six or twenty-seven, limping on a foot half shot away years before by a shotgun blast.

Missou quieted a little and tried to look sober at their entrance, and John, yawning and stretching, got up and slouched to the bar.

"Whiskey!" he said, but the bartender was too busy with the new customers who had entered to hear him. John struck the bar with the heel of his palm and roared: "Whiskey, do ye hear, or would you rather I parted your hair with a Thirty-Six-caliber comb?"

The bartender stopped and looked at him without favor. He set a glass out and knocked it sliding down the bar with the back of his hand. He hooked a jug of trade whiskey from under the bar and John stopped him.

"Not that!" He pointed at a fancy decanter bottle of Old Haversill bourbon that occupied the place of glory on the back bar, a showpiece, intended not for drinking but for style. "That!"

The bartender couldn't believe his ears.

"That?" he asked, pointing to a half-gone bottle of cheaper whiskey.

"No," said John. He moved a step toward the middle of the room, his right shoulder dipped, and there was a backward slouch of his body. A Navy exploded with a finger of powder flame over the edge of the bar and the fancy bottle of Old Haversill stood neckless with bits of glass and cork zinging the air. "That!"

The explosion had stopped every other sound in the room. As everyone stared, Comanche John chewed, and spat, and reholstered his Navy.

"Gittin' so's a Californy man can't make himself understood speakin' the English lang'age. Country full up with Abolitionists and draft dodgers. The *English* lang'age? . . . got to talk to 'em in *Colt* lang'age."

With awed deference the bartender set down the decapitated bottle of Old Haversill, and John poured from its shattered neck. "Messy job," he complained. "Putting no glass in the bottles these days. Cheapness showing up everywhar.

109

Time was ye could nick off a bottle clean as an undertaker's chin."

"Say!" cried Missou after holding his breath a long ten seconds. "That was shootin'!"

"Oh, I keep my eye sharp. Weren't much, though, compared to the man that taught me."

"Who in tarnation *taught* you?"

"Nobody but the one and gen-u-wine Jimmy Dale!"

"Jimmy Dale from Californy? Why I seen him one time. It was in Placerville, the vigilantes was after him, they was combing the country after him, and one night in he comes, straight into camp, all alone, riding a big bay horse, and he climbed off in front of everybody and walked inside the Star West Saloon. Had a brace of pearl-handled Navies on his hips, and one of them German needle-fire repeating rifles under his arm, and not a cowardly son of 'em raised a finger."

John lowered his voice, looking around. "Yep, I believe it. I seen Jimmy a heap of times. I seen something no other man has seen. I seen him *dead*. I did. And I buried him, rolled up in his quilts, his hat over his face, and an ounce of bushwhackin' vigilante lead in his back. We rode down the deep gulch together, Jimmy and me. We took things as they come, the gold and the lead both. Share and share alike, that was our motto."

Missou almost swallowed his tobacco from amazement. "Say! What you trying to tell us? You must be. . . ."

"Who I be and who I *might* be are subjects that's been discussed by some live men and lots of dead ones."

Overfelt had been trying to remember and now he snapped his fingers in a sign of recognition. "Sure, now I know where I saw you before . . . Vermont Bar, year of 'Fifty-Eight. You're Comanche John."

Under his breath, tapping a boot heel, Missou sang:

John started out for Singleshot
With a pal named Jimmy Dale
And just for some excitement
They robbed the Union mail. . . .

"Never you mind that," said John. "Folks hereabouts have got me buried over in I-de-ho, and I'm just as happy in my grave." Then he added: "Mite gant, though. Could do with a weight of gold on me. I heered of you boys, that's why I come. Figured we might just maybe. . . ."

"I don't know," said Overfelt. "Sometimes a man carves out too much reputation for himself."

"Trying to be considerate," John said. "Trying to play square. Don't like to move in with a gang of my own and upset the good thing ye have. Rather jine ye. You're men of my style and cut of my cloth. Gold enough for all. Gold flowing like she is from Chinee Gulch, no good reason why we shouldn't be able to git rich and ree-tire to live the good life like country squires, and even run for Congress, when the war's over and this territory takes her place amongst the glorious states of the Confed'racy!"

"Hoorah for Jeff Davis!" said Missou. "That's talk I like to hear."

John drank with Missou and Billy Step-And-A-Half. He drank less than he appeared to—when they became drunk enough, he wasn't drunk at all. Others joined them. In a back room they played poker. Missou went to sleep and snored. He fell out of his chair and lay on the floor, still snoring. Big, rough Hoss Noon cursed him and kicked him in the ribs without succeeding in awakening him. Then he drew a Navy, and cocked it, and aimed it at his head. Nobody said anything, but with a shrug of regret he put the Navy back. "Should kill him. Man can't hold his likker. Bound to give you away sometime. Should never have took him in."

A man called Little Frenchy smiled with rabbit teeth and said: "He's here firs', don' you remembaire?"

"Well, you listen to me, he'll go waltzing into the Montana House once too often sometime, and. . . ." He finished the thought by pointing a forefinger at his temple like a gun, and using his thumb to simulate the falling hammer. "He'll disobey the *big* boss once too often sometime and that'll be all for Missou."

"What's wrong with the Montana House?" John asked. "If ye ask me that's a fancy establishment."

"Fancy's no word for it, only we stay out."

"Why?"

Hoss Noon let out a loud, braying laugh. "Listen to him. He wants to know why we don't go in the Montana House. That's a question that's been troubling some of the other boys, too. Well, the answer is, we do go in, but only for a drink, and then we get out. Point is we don't hang around there. Why? Because it's orders. The sheriff ain't after us and we're all living mighty high, staying out of the Montana House and taking orders. Curiosity," Hoss added with the manner of one inventing a new and apt remark, "kilt the cat!"

"Then," said John, "I'll not be the one to go ag'in' established principle. Good enough for you, it's good enough for me. Share and share alike, that's my motto."

VI

"FEMALE AMUSEMENT"

He slept in a shanty with Hoss Noon, Frenchy, and Huckven. It was dark when he got there, and he had an uncomfortable moment in the morning when Huckven sat up and had a first bleary look at him, but he did not recognize John as the man who had covered him with a Navy that night up the gulch.

"They tell me you claim to be Comanche John," Huckven said, parting his stringy blond mustaches off to one side and the other. "Well, I knew Comanche John, shacked up with him in Utah, and robbed coaches with him in the Sierras, and you don't look nothing like him. Besides, the Comanche's dead, shot by a sheriff's posse in Oregon Gulch down in Coloraydo."

"That's peculiar," said John. "I got right hyar in my pocket a certificate saying I was hung in I-de-ho City. And I was hung in Yallerjack, too. How many graveyards I got fighting over me, anyhow?"

"That 'un they hung in I-de-ho City was an imposter. Some men'll do anything to get folks to admire 'em. Even git hung. So I ain't admiring you, or giving you an inch of ground just because you claim to be Comanche John."

He had no more trouble with Huckven. He had no trouble

with any of them. They were an indolent, drunken lot, but fair company. Then one morning, with dawn just on its way and the camp quiet, Overfelt awakened them with word that a task awaited them in the direction of Last Chance.

They rode all day, slept in an abandoned wickiup near Green Cañon, and waited most of the next day by a rough side road about twelve miles to the west of Last Chance Gulch. All John knew was that the road led back into the mountains to Reddow, a hard-rock camp where several outcroppings of "rotten quartz" were being worked by means of hand mortars, amalgamating pans, and vanners, the amalgamating pans catching most of the gold and horn silver through its willingness to join with mercury which later was distilled leaving a silver-gold sponge, the vanners making a rich lead-silver concentrate of the rest, and this was sacked and hauled by wagon to Fort Benton 200 miles to the north, then by river steamboat to St. Louis, and then by rail to the Eastern seaboard where sailing ships transported it to the smelters of Saxony or Wales.

After waiting until late in the afternoon, a freight outfit consisting of three wagons and a long, jerk-line string of mules came into sight. There were two teamsters and two men riding guard, but not a shot was fired. Masked, with guns drawn, Comanche John and most of the others waited at a distance of forty or fifty yards while Overfelt, Hoss Noon, and a young fellow called Oregon rode in leading a pack horse, explaining their mission.

The freight boss laughed bitterly and said they'd play hell hauling off much of the concentrate, and play further hell selling it when they did, but Overfelt ordered the wagons unloaded and unearthed the thing he was looking for, a cache of gold and silver sponge.

"He was damned well informed!" said John.

"You stick with me," said Missou. "We're *always* well informed."

Two days later, in New Boston, John got as his split a poke of gold, regular Chinee Gulch dust, the sponge having been disposed of he knew not how.

Again there was nothing to do but take his ease in one saloon or another. He dropped a few hints concerning the claims that had been staked on White Pine bottoms and learned nothing. They had been staked, like the robbery had been performed, on orders. He tried to learn the identity of the big boss, and failed. The Montana House, however, was forbidden ground. The gang was not to be seen loitering there. So one evening, there he was, in the Montana, a theater, bar, and gambling house, probably the largest in the territory.

He played faro and won a little, and three card monte and lost a little. In the theater, an orchestra consisting of a cornet, a violin, and a harp commenced to play. The theater offered standing room and some boxes with painted screen fronts where the new-rich tycoons of Chinee Gulch and the Shauvegan could drink champagne with their women friends and see without being seen.

After half an hour of orchestra music, some curtains parted revealing a tiny, gilt-arched stage and the show commenced. It was a rowdy show presenting the same performance over and over in songs, dances, and comic dialogues.

Then, with a flourish, a man in tight checkerboard trousers, a corset-fitting coat, a cane, and a high, mouse-colored silk hat advanced to the middle of the stage and announced in clear, tenor tones the feature attraction of the evening, direct from St. Louis, New York, and Paris, France, the Songbird of the Seine, Mademoiselle Louise

115

Devereux, La Belle Gants de Soie.

Mademoiselle Devereux proved to be on the large side, but well-curved, buxom, brunette, and beautiful. She wore a white gown covered with spangles, and lace gloves to her elbows. In mid-stage she waited until the crowd quieted, then posturing, clasping her hands, with a French accent forgotten after the first measure, she sang:

> **Thees handful of earth do we send you,**
> **Thees handful of earth did we save,**
> **This earth from your dear Molly's grave. . . .**

Men wept, and, when she had finished, they fairly tore the place down in their enthusiasm. She returned to mid-stage and was showered by gold pieces and nuggets. A Negro scurried around gathering the gold into a cigar box as she returned for repeated encores. "More, more!" cried the audience with fresh showers of gold. She waited until the last available nugget had been tossed, then a painted flat representing a log cabin with an improbable waterfall was carried on stage, and she returned gowned in velvet and sang "The Cabin Where the Old Folks Died". Again she was applauded with more gold, but men familiar with her act from other nights started shouting: "'Natchez Song'! 'Natchez Song'!"

To this she responded by pulling her gown over her head, and, amid the roar of the audience, she walked around shaking her hips, slapping her hindquarters, garbed in nothing except cream-colored tights.

"Whoopee!" shouted John with the rest. "Hoorah for La Belle Gants de Soie!"

She now cut loose with a rowdy song popular in the river towns of the lower Mississippi:

What kind o' drawers do the white girls wear?
What kind o' drawers do the rich girls wear?
Pink and lace worth two dollar a pair,
That's what, honey, mine!
What kind o' drawers do the yaller gals wear?
What kind o' drawers do the brown gals wear?
None at all, they just go bare,
That's what, honey, mine!

Comanche John had squeezed through the crowd until he could almost hang his nose over the stage. He was so close he could smell the perfume she wore. She was the most beautiful woman he had ever seen, and the best scented. But even as he gained his place of vantage, he was caught in a wash of the shoving crowd and carried away to be pinned against the wall. At his back was one of the private boxes. Its sliding front was partially open; he saw it was unoccupied. He climbed inside. It contained a spindle-legged gilt table and four spindly gilt chairs. He sat down in one of the chairs, tilted back in it, put his jackboots on the table, spurted tobacco juice on the floor, and watched in style. Then, of a sudden, he noticed that La Belle Gants de Soie was staring at him.

He arose, swept off his battered slouch hat, thrust one jackboot far out, bent the other knee, and bowed. She smiled, reached far out with her silken-gloved hand, and blew a kiss to him.

"Champagne!" roared John, beating the table with his fist.

A Chinese boy must have been awaiting just those words for scarcely had he uttered them when the door at his back popped open, and there he was with the bottle and two glasses.

"You would like female amusement?" asked the boy.

"Just leave that bottle. I'm *gittin'* female amusement."

Comanche John opened the bottle by knocking its neck off with his Navy. The champagne was warm and wild. He drank the top two inches to save it. It got all bubbly up his nose. He was sneezing it when the door opened again and this time a short, extremely powerful, gorilla-built man looked in on him.

"By grab," said John. "I would welcome a visitor, but not you."

"Get out," said the man. He had a peculiar accent. "Go, leave."

John arose. "You telling me to git?"

"Boss said go, leave."

"What boss?"

"Malloy."

Walker Malloy, that would be. Walker Malloy, owner of the Montana House, part owner of the K-Y freight outfit, share owner in half a dozen placer mines, representative in the territorial legislature that just recently had met in Bannack City.

"Malloy, hey?" said John. He was crafty now, for this was what he had come to learn. "Ain't I good enough for him? Ain't shaved, ain't pomaded my whiskers?"

"Get out!" said the short man, letting his hand fall to the butt of the double Derringer thrust in the sash at his waist.

The threat proved a mistake. He had no chance to draw the gun. John's right-hand Navy was out. "Dance, dang ye!" he whooped. "Jig high, kick your heels!" He fired. The bullet split one side of the man's boot. It stung his foot and sent him hopping and grimacing, holding the foot in his hand. John whooped, fired again, tearing half the sole from the other boot as he came down. "I'll show ye who gits! Maybe you're for Malloy, but I'm for me, and do you know who I be? I'm a ring-tailed ripper from the Rawhide Mountains. I'm a mangy old he-wolf from Orofino Gulch. In summer I range with the mountain lions, and, when winter comes, I den up with the grizzly b'ars. Some folks ask what I stand for and what are my principles. Waal, I'm for sidemeat and corn likker, I'm for slavery in the territories, and Jeff Davis for President!"

The man fled, limping on his bullet-shredded boots. The air was blue and raw from powder smoke. No one paid more than passing heed to the pistol shots as they cheered La Belle Gants de Soie, and now she was singing again. John had a drink of the fancy wine and sat down to listen. He caught sight of the man again, limping around the far side of the room, stopping at a booth where a lean, tall, very handsome man was seated, one polished Spanish boot notched on the edge of the table, hands clasped across his silver and tan fancy vest, a long, slim cigar scissored in his teeth.

"Why, I'd reckon that's him!" said John. "Mister Walker Malloy himself. Representative in the territorial legislature. Got his hand in everything in law, in mining, and in robbery, too. Even itching for the White Pine Valley! Poor damn' farmers, willing to run 'em out of their homes."

La Belle concluded. The stage was taken over by a buck-and-wing in blackface. Malloy got to his feet and went out. John waited, jackboots on the table, black slouch hat over his eyes, chaw of tobacco in one cheek, the champagne at his right hand. There was a rap, and when he said—"Come in."—it was not Walker Malloy, as he expected, but La Belle Gants de Soie. He got his boots down and almost swallowed his tobacco. "La Belle. . . ."

"Hush!" she whispered with her finger to her lips. "Don' let heem hear you. Don' let heem know I am here!"

"Let who know?" asked John.

"That man!" She wrung her hands. "Oh, how I fear heem! That man . . . Walker Malloy."

"By grab, you don't need to be skeered of Malloy or anybody else as long as I'm around."

"Oh, John!" she said, weeping with her cheek pressed against his chest. "John, will you help me?"

"How do you know my name is John?"

"But you are famous! You are the great Comanche John!"

John, supporting her, asked: "How many more folks knows I'm Comanche John?"

"But no one! Only me. In California I saw your picture. Then, when I saw you. . . ."

By grab, John was thinking, *I am famous and women do have a way of taking to me! There was that Blackfeet gal a year ago, and the Widow Cobb, and now La Belle Gants de Soie herself.* He said: "So ye be well acquainted with Walker Malloy?"

"He got me here. He promised a lot of theengs." Every so often she would sound very French. "All the way from New Orleans he breeng me! He promised I would seeng in ze opera. And look, this place, thees cheap variety theater!"

"Thar, thar now! Don't you cry about it because I'm here to help ye!"

"You will! What will you do?"

"Waal, there's several courses of action, but we better plan things out. He's a mighty important man, Malloy. Representative in that damn' Yankee legislature down in Bannack, gold claims, fancy clothes, important friends. Yep, we got to go easy. Larn a few things about him, whar he lives, whar he keeps his valuables, all that sort of truck."

"I will do anything!" she whispered. "Any-zeeng."

VII

"SECRET MISSION"

Comanche John drank champagne with La Belle Gants de Soie. After she left, he had a fling at faro. He wandered all over the lower floor of the big building, getting the lay of the ground. Some stairs led above and he would have climbed those, but seated on guard, a sawed-off shotgun at hand, was the short, hunched, powerful man who he had caused to dance in the theater. He had new boots on, John noticed, but judging by his mean expression he still did not feel good about it. The type who harbored a grudge, Belle had called him Max the Ape. It was a good name, it fit him, he looked like an ape with his slanty forehead and his thrust-out mouth and chin, and those arms, away too long and strong for a man of his height.

John stood by the monte game and looked around. At the head of the stairs and to the left was a small balcony, and there, watching him, was Walker Malloy. His hang-out was there, on the upper floor, his "apartment" Belle had called it. John itched to visit his apartment and have a talk with him, and thought over all sorts of excuses to get there, and what he would say after he *did* get there. But Max the Ape would be hard to convince. He decided to see the parson.

It was now about midnight. "Ho-ho-hum!" yawned John.

"Reckon this be a quiet night. Might as well hit the shucks."

He left. He had an idea he was being followed. He went to the shack. Missou, Huckven, none of the men was there. He went straight on and crawled through the rear window of the mission. "Parson!" he said into the darkness. The parson was not there. He got his horse from the feed corral and rode toward the White Pine. He did not get there. A man was riding from the region of the old fur post, skulking along, following some brush shadow, and John, hunting shadow of his own, waited for him. The man proved to be Wally Snite.

He gave Wally Snite a quarter mile and followed. He lost sight of him among the outlying shanties of New Boston. Acting on a hunch, he rode at a gallop along one of the gulch-side streets, dismounted, and took a path to the rear door of the Montana House. He stopped, hunkered in the shadows, got his breath.

Scarcely half a minute passed and there was Wally Snite, on foot, sneaking into view, pausing to look all around, and then climbing some rear stairs to the second floor of the Montana.

"Yellabelly! Yankee!" Snite wasn't a Yankee, he had the talk of a Missouri man, but John always considered him a Yankee by inclination. "Told 'em not to trust him! Wouldn't listen to me. But it's me got to get their land grant back!"

He considered following Snite up the stairs. He didn't. He walked all around the building, looking at the upper floor windows. They told him nothing. He had a look at the crowd inside, thinking that Snite, an avowed temperance man, might just be sneaking off for a round with the bottle. He was not there. All this took time; perhaps half an hour had passed. He went back to the rear. Just as he arrived, the door at the top of the stairs opened and men were moving around. He retreated and hunkered in the shadows to watch. One of those men was Max the Ape, and there were two more. They were struggling with something. Tall man, that was Huckven. They were carrying the limp body of a man.

He followed them, keeping a safe distance. He decided they were headed for a certain place around some outbuildings and circled to intercept them. He waited several minutes. No sound. He had been wrong. He had lost them. He blamed himself for not keeping at their heels. He had a good hunch who the dead man was, but he had wanted to be sure. He poked back through the outbuildings and almost stumbled over the body. It was Wally Snite and he had been shot in the back.

"Of course!" said John. "Used him for what he was worth, stole the paper for 'em, probably thought they'd make him rich. Instead, all he collected was a half ounce of lead. That's how it is drawing cyards in another man's game."

John left him there. He went to the shanty. Missou was drunk and asleep. John could not stand the sound and smell of him, so he carried his robes to the open and slept there.

He awoke ill-tempered. It was that fancy wine of the night before. He felt better after dipping his head in the creek, and better yet after breakfast and a chaw. The parson was still not at the mission, but starting again for the White Pine he met the old man on his mule about a mile from camp.

"Whar's Wally Snite?" were John's first words.

The parson jerked and said: "His woman's been wondering."

"Waal, you go congratulate her because she's a widow."

"Ye didn't . . . ?"

"Of course I didn't. His *friends* did it. Walker Malloy, and that one they call Max the Ape."

"What are you talking about?"

"Just that. He stole it for 'em. The grant. Stole it and

burned the place down, I'd reckon, so it wouldn't be missed. Went to visit 'em last night. To collect maybe . . . well, he collected. Lead in the back. So Malloy's got your deed. But I promised ye I'd git it back, and I'll git it back."

"How can you get it back?" moaned the parson. "You'll never get it back. We'll have to fight 'em, that's all."

"Mayhap ye will, but it'll be better to fight with the legal title than without it."

"How could you get it back? You'll get shot."

"No-o, I won't. I got idees, Parson, and I got cleverness. When you're up again' a smart man like Malloy, only thing is to be smarter than he is."

"John, you're fast with a Navy, and you're trueblue, but smartness ain't one o' your qualities."

"Next thing you'll say is women don't like me neither. What'd ye say if I told ye that last night I was picked and chosen by La Belle Gants de Soie?"

"I'd say beware of that woman. She's Malloy's woman and she'll lead ye to disaster."

John rode off muttering: "Blamed old rooster! Jealous of me. Saying things about Belle. I'll show him whether that woman's ashamed of me."

The warning, however, continued to bother him, and that night, when he managed a meeting with Belle, he said: "I might as well tell ye, gal, I'm here on a secret mission. Yep, I be, and I intend to listen to none of your talk about one of the finest men in the territory, and I mean Walker Malloy!"

When she was gone, John said: "That's the ticket! Let her carry that to him. When ye go after a man like Malloy, got to be smart, got to be wary."

He watched for Malloy. An hour passed. The ape guarded the stairs. He slouched up, and, using his body to hide his action from the rest of the room, he drew a Navy and said: "Climb!"

The ape had been watching him, but the sudden appearance of the gun was a surprise. He sprang to his feet with his short, straddle legs working like released springs; he opened his mouth and closed it like a fish. He had the double-gun, but he did not point it; he put it down, without a word turned, and climbed the stairs.

"That's the ticket," said John, close behind. "Don't look back. Don't argue. Just climb. Malloy's yonder, in his rooms, and that's whar you're taking me."

They reached the top of the stairs and walked straight on through a hall lighted by candles in bracket lamps. The ape stopped at a closed door.

"Don't rap," said John. "Don't say a word. Ye might have a signal worked out and it'd only git ye kilt. Just open."

The ape swung the door open revealing Walker Malloy seated behind a table, writing in a ledger.

"What the devil?" said Malloy, rising to his feet. He saw Comanche John and the leveled Navy. He froze with a hand resting on the pearl-handled gun at his waist, his face stony, his eyes as narrow and hard as twin pieces of quartz.

"Visitor," said John nudging the ape aside and going in past him. He caught the door with his boot heel and kicked it shut in the ape's face. He leaned against the door and bolted it. He thrust the Navy back in its holster. He chewed and looked around the room furnished as no room he had seen this side of Salt Lake. "Say, this is something! This is something. This is quality. By grab, this is style!"

Malloy decided to smile. He did it in the brittle, correct way he did everything. "Thank you!"

"Yep, *style*." He kept looking around the room. There were some shelves stacked with papers, the grant might be there, and there was a black metal strongbox on the desk, it might be there. There was another room to the left, an archway covered by a velvet drape. No windows in the room—but straight overhead was a skylight. A man could lower himself from that skylight and nigh put his feet on the table.

"What do you want?" asked Malloy with an edgy voice.

"Spittoon, wouldn't want to douse this carpet. Say, this is a carpet!" He located the spittoon, took very careful aim, and hit it. "Lots of folks wouldn't try a shot like that, but chawin' tobacco is like doing anything else, if it's worth doing at all, it's worth doing right. I. . . ."

Malloy sat down again, sticking his boots far out. They were fine boots, the best Spanish, very long and narrow. He wore paisley-mix trousers, the real English cloth, a white linen shirt, a black string tie. His hair was reddish and slightly gray at the temples, but he was not more than thirty-two or thirty-three years old. He had long bloodless fingers and a nervous way of picking things up and laying them down.

"You have your guts," he said. "Walking in here like this! I admire guts!"

"Thankee."

"But that might not stop me killing you."

"Could ye?"

"I could. What do you want?"

"You're an important man, Malloy. Representative in legislature, mine owner, businessman, head boss of the worst gang of varmints in the territory. Now, what would ye say if *I* said ye were wasting your talents, monkey-puddling around with small-bore stuff? What would ye say if I told ye I came here not to take a hand in robbery, but for one purpose, and that to find a man of talent to take over the whole of Montana Territory for the gov'ment, to run it for 'em, to be paid a legal commission for running it so's he couldn't help but make himself the richest, powerfullest man in the whole Nor'west."

"The government?" Malloy was ready to laugh, but something about John's eyes stopped him.

"Not Lincoln's variety of gov'ment. Not by a jugful. I mean the real, legal gov'ment, as soon as the Territory of Montana, together with Oregon, I-de-ho, and Washington jines with Jeff Davis and the Confed'racy."

Malloy was interested. He struck a patent match and waited for the chemical to stop showering sparks before applying it to his cigar. He puffed and watched while John fumbled deep in his homespuns and came out with a folder almost worn out from long carrying. Malloy took it, opened it, and looked at it. Then he stopped John from saying any more and addressed the draped doorway.

"All right, Huck, you can come out."

John stopped chewing and watched as the draperies moved and Huckven ambled, tall and loose-jointed, into view with a gun in his hand.

"Put it up," said Malloy, and Huckven did, reluctantly, his lips twisted down.

John said, jerking his head at Huckven: "He told ye thar was something wrong with me being here, didn't he? Warned ye. Well, Huck is no ordinary man. He ain't taken in like the rest. He knew Comanche John wasn't the type to jine with a gang of road agents and take orders. And I ain't. I'm here for a purpose. The great. . . ."

"Never mind," Malloy said softly through his teeth. "Huckven, let us alone." He waited, drumming the table with his nervous fingers until Huckven was through the door and the door closed. "Keep this between us. What is your secret mission?"

He had not said secret mission to Malloy. He had said it to

La Belle Gants de Soie. It jolted him, and it made him wince. *Dratted parson!* he thought. The parson was always turning up right about people. He said: "Yep, as that paper says I'm with that secret patriotic organization of the South, the Knights of the Golden Circle. I'm roving representative with the full power of the control conclave behind me. We be gittin' ready to move. Knights in Californy, Nevada, I-de-ho, Coloraydo, Oregon, men, all trained, guns ready, plan set, Army style."

Malloy, cool and smiling, said: "One morning they'll just wake up and there it will be?"

"Thar it'll be. We got a general heading it. Real general . . . Mexican war. Colonels, majors, everything."

"I have a surprise for you. I'm from the North."

"I know. As for you being *for* the North, I think not. You be *for* Walker Malloy."

Malloy did not argue with that. He said: "Why would you want me to take over the country?"

"Because you could make it produce. Right now the freight, trade and gold buying is all Yankee. Things have got to keep moving, but for the South. Got to git the gold to the Southern buyers. They need it desperate bad to keep buying guns in Europe. Gold will win the war. Have to keep the miners working. Have to make mining more profitable under the Confed'racy than under the Union, otherwise the miners will rise up and run us out. Agree?"

"Agree!"

"You're the man for us, Malloy. You'd keep it moving. You'd take over when we run these damn' Yankee gold buyers and flour merchants out. You take their profit. Only fair. Profit you earn. When the war is over, they get their businesses back, but before then I wouldn't be amazed if Mister Walker Malloy mightn't make himself one of the richest men in the whole Nor'west!"

VIII

"WHAT A SMART MAN CAN DO"

No longer did Comanche John bed down on the floor of the shack. He slept in the Montana, in a room with a bed. He had breakfast prepared by Walker Malloy's Chinese cook. He had credit at the bar. There was an afternoon show that he watched from the private luxury of a box. He received a visit from La Belle who he pretended to take into his confidence, telling her exactly what he wanted carried on to Walker Malloy. He sat with his jackboots on the spindly little table, tilted back on the rear legs of an equally spindly chair. Things were fine for his comfort. Things were going top riffle. It showed what a man could do when he used his brain.

That night with Malloy downstairs watching the games he found a fire hole and climbed to the roof. The night was cool. The moon was under clouds, but he could see. The roof was flat and slanting, covered with a layer of gravel to help shed the rain. It was broken by chimneys, ventilators, and the skylight above Malloy's office. He walked to the skylight.

The office was dark. The skylight had been lifted on a prop pole. A slight current of warm air drifted up carrying the odors of perfume, liquor, and Cuban cigar. He was in no hurry. He crouched on one knee listening. It seemed safe enough.

He strapped his Navies more tightly around him, pulled off his jackboots, carefully lifted the near side of the skylight as far as its hinges would allow, and lowered himself inside.

He hung by his hands, swinging his feet, groping for the table. It was farther below than he thought. He dropped. The table was there. Alighting, he knocked something to the floor. It struck with a slight *rattle* on the rug. He crouched on the table, looking about him at the blackness, listening. He could hear a muffled mutter of voices and the orchestra in the theater below, but no one in the room.

He got off the table, groped, found the box of patent matches, struck one. It was the candle he had knocked off. He lighted it.

Barefoot, he walked, looking behind furniture, behind the drapes, inside the little parlor, and in a third room containing nothing except a chair and a bed where Malloy slept. He tried the doors. They were locked, but he bolted them, too. Then, working systematically, he searched the room. He took everything out, examined it, and put it back again. He worked for at least an hour. At last all that was left was the strongbox and it was locked. He lifted it. It was very heavy. A box that heavy contained gold. Using his Bowie, he managed to get its lock turned. It contained several buckskin pokes of gold dust with the initials I.J.R. burned in, also the greater portion of the gold and silver sponge they had taken in the robbery near Last Chance, some papers, and a quantity of greenbacks, but not the parchment he was looking for.

He put it all back, closed and locked the box, and pressed out some of the nicks he had made with the Bowie. He had a last look around, but he knew that his search had been fruitless.

Now he was presented with the problem of getting out. There were outside windows from both the bedroom and the parlor, but mosquito cloth was tacked over them, and it would be a long drop to the ground. He decided to go back through the skylight.

He unbolted the doors, placed a chair on the table and stood on it, but the skylight was still about eighteen inches beyond his reach. Steadying himself with one hand on the ceiling, he climbed to the back of the chair, stood with a momentarily shaky balance, and got hold of the sill. Hanging there, he hooked the chair with his toes, swung it off the table, and dropped it to the floor.

After long quiet it struck with what seemed to be a fearful *thud* and *crash*. He chinned himself, almost lost balance and toppled back, but a final effort brought him forward on his knees with his hands on the rough gravel of the roof, and suddenly he realized that there was a man beside him, and a gun's cold, round muzzle was pressed against the back of his head.

He remained on all fours. He did not move.

"Don't try nothing, Comanche!" It was the voice of Huckven. "Don't try nothing, because it'd be a pleasure for me to kill you!"

IX

"A ROUGH ROPE AND A GOOD DROP"

He saw other men now, on the roof, and a light came on in Malloy's office.

"Waal," said John to Huckven, "I see ye had some help. Good idee to have help when ye go out for the Comanche."

Huckven, standing back and sneering through his stringy mustache, said: "I didn't need 'em. I'd tooken you myself, *by* myself, if I'd had my way. I'd have outdrawn you and killed you, only the boss said no."

Clip Overfelt emerged from hiding behind a chimney and walked over with moonlight flashing on the gun in his hand.

"Walk, Comanche!" said Huckven.

Overfelt said: "Aren't you taking his guns?"

"Hell with 'em. I hope he draws. I only hope it!"

"Take his guns!"

"You take 'em."

John said: "Lemme unbuckle 'em."

"Keep your hands clear!" Overfelt, careful not to come in front of Huckven, stepped in gingerly and plucked the Navies from the holsters.

"My boots!" said John.

"Put 'em on."

They waited for him, and walked him to the fire hole. Two other men were below. One was George Finch, a short, stocky man wearing a deputy's badge. The other was Max the Ape.

"By grab," said John with satisfaction, "they do git their forces out when they go to take the Comanche."

Malloy was seated in his office, a fresh cigar in his teeth.

"What were you searching for?" he asked when John walked in.

"Why I had to investigate. Knights of the Golden Circle, ye know. Make sure ye was the man. . . ."

"Jig's up. You're not here for the Knights. What are you here for?"

"I told ye. . . ."

In fury Malloy sprang from his chair. He came around the table with his short-barreled, pearl-handled pistol in his hand. He cried: "I ask a question, I want an answer. The right answer. No lie, but the right answer!"

John tried to retreat and was brought up short by the thrust of Huckven's gun in his back. He tried to get his hands up to take the blow he saw coming, but Malloy brought the gun up and around in a sudden arc, clipping him on the side of the skull, and the next John knew he was down on hands and knees, his ears deaf and ringing.

Instinctively he tried to get to his feet. He fell face forward with his mouth open and his eyes glazed. He heard Malloy shout: "Get him off the floor! Put him in the chair! Get his hands tied!"

He knew everything they were doing, but he was unable to move. He knew when they dragged him to a chair and tied his forearms to the arm rests. Malloy was still shouting questions at him. His voice came in waves with pain. He could hear the words, but they seemed meaningless. Finally Malloy gave up and went somewhere. A long time seemed to pass. John came awake thinking it must at least be the next afternoon, but the room was still lit by candles, and not a hint of morning yet came through the window overhead.

"Looking for Malloy?" Huckven asked. "He'll be back. With the judge. The legal, elected judge. Union judge, the Honorable Cincinnatus Harrison. Nothing old Cincy would rather do than hang a Johnny Reb. Especially one on the prowl for the Knights of the Golden Circle. You picked the wrong camp. This must be a Union camp."

He turned his head; it pained him but he turned it. He saw the ape, and George Finch, the deputy. Apparently they'd been waiting a considerable time, for Finch had made himself comfortable on the divan.

John tried to speak. His mouth was thick and thirsty. "I need a drink."

"The hell you do!" said Huckven.

Finch opened his eyes and said: "Give him a drink."

"Who in hell's giving orders around here?"

"Give him a drink!"

So Huckven got a dipper of water and held it to John's lips while he drank, but he got weary before the water was gone and, dumping the remainder in John's face, tossed the dipper back in its bucket.

"Thankee," said John.

"Don't thank me, I'd as soon leave it war pizen."

A door had opened and closed, there was a stir of air, and he heard voices. They were in the parlor. One was Malloy. Another had a pompous orator's way of talking.

"Speak of the devil," said the deputy, sitting up on the edge of the divan, yawning and rubbing his hair, and John knew that the pompous voice belonged to Judge Cincinnatus Harrison.

He heard Malloy say: "I quite agree, and that's what I've been trying to tell you all the time. It has to be done legally. Everything has to be done legally."

"We'll give him a fair, impartial, public trial, and hang him afterward. But I strongly suggest the charge be murder and robbery and the Knights of the Circle be left out of it. There are entirely too many Confederate sympathizers in New Boston to divide the town."

"Agreed."

"Evidence?"

"You'll have your evidence."

Malloy then lowered his voice and there was a considerable span of conversation lost to John, then the judge said: "Indeed, yes! If that fur company grant is in your possession, by all means move them off the ground at once. Why, man, your mining equipment will be here and you haven't even test-drilled the ground."

So John had been correct concerning the deep gravel deposit. The White Pine held millions for an outfit with the brains and the capital to take it.

I've really ruint things now, thought John. *The parson should never have sent for me. Shouldn't have tried to out-figure Malloy. Should just have shot him.*

Judge Cincinnatus Harrison came in and looked at him. The judge was a soft-looking man of fifty, his face red and pouchy. Tonight he was neither more drunk nor more sober than usual. He wore black serge, its front stained by food, drink, and cigar ash. In his hand he carried a rolled-up umbrella. No one had ever seen Harrison open the umbrella; he used it as a cane; it added to his dignity.

He burped and said: "Is this the defendant? I don't

want to hang the wrong man."

Hoss Noon and Oregon were in the hall, and Hoss said to Finch: "You're supposed to deputize us."

"How in hell can I deputize you? The sheriff has to do that and he's in Hangtown."

"I'll deputize you," said Harrison. "Lift your right hands. I declare you deputies of the court empowered to enforce its authority within the boundaries of the Territory of Montana."

Hoss was drunk as always. He whooped and kicked his boots in the air and said: "Whoopee! Always wanted to be a deppity. They's six men in this camp I'm aiming to shoot."

Things had come to life on the lower floor. From everywhere John could hear the boots and voices of men. In the distance someone was beating a drum. Oregon went to look and came back saying: "That's Foolish Mike Peabody again. I wonder how he got wind of it so soon? His shack's a mile down the gulch."

Foolish Mike was sort of a town crier who went around beating his drum whenever there was important news, passing the hat for small color. Out of money and lacking other news, Foolish Mike was not above inventing Union or Confederate victories, either of which paid off well from New Boston's partisan population, but tonight he had real news, and they could hear his hoarse voice accentuated by the boom of the drum: "They caught him, they caught him!" *Boom! Boom!* "Comanche John." *Boom!* "He'll rob no more. They'll hang him." *Boom! Boom!* "He robbed the sluice at Whiskey Gulch. Killed three men, killed three men. Shot 'em down in co-old blood."

He came booming closer and closer until they could feel the impact of the bass drum from the street below, and there he went on reciting the details of the Whiskey Gulch sluice robbery a month before, a foul piece of business in which three miners had been shot from ambush.

John, rolling his head around to get the ache from it, said: "Ain't I guilty of enough without inventing things? I never robbed a sluice in my life. Sluice robbing to my mind is the next lowest thing to slave stealing."

"How about ambush?" Finch asked.

"Waal, how about it? Ask Huckven about it. He's a man with more experience with ambush than anybody else in this room."

A man came in breathlessly and said: "Judge says bring the prisoner before they tear the place down."

Under Finch's direction the rawhide thongs were unfastened, freeing John from the chair. Huckven kept him covered. "Tie his hands behind him," Finch said, and the harsh rawhide was used again. Looking around, Finch asked: "Where are his guns?"

"Guns?" Huckven and Overfelt looked at each other.

"Yes, his guns! Do you think you'll get away with them, sell them and pocket the money? Like hell you will. This is a trial and the guns are the murder weapons. They're exhibit A. So get 'em and have 'em at the jail."

"And be damn' careful not to tamper with 'em!" John called at Huckven's back. "You git them Navies out o' kilter, I'll come around and blast six cubits out of your middle."

"You'll be dead and six foot under with your neck stretched out longer'n a whooping crane's. You'll do nothing to nobody!"

The rawhide thongs hurt him when he moved. "Mighty tight, mighty painful," he said.

"Mighty dead the three you bushwhacked at Whiskey Gulch," said Overfelt in his tight-lipped way, prodding him with the gun muzzle in the back.

"You ought to know!"

"We found the gold on you."

"Ye did?"

"Exhibit B."

"Why, ye plan fast, ye do fast. I knew it! I knew I should have stayed north of this camp of New Boston."

They walked him down the stairs toward the jail. The air was close from the smell of the crowd packed on the floor below. "Make way, make way!" the ape was saying, pushing through, shouldering men this way and that. "Don't touch the prisoner."

Men filled the lower rooms, they stood on card tables, they boosted themselves on the bar to get a glimpse of him. "It's him, it's the Comanche!" they were saying. "I seen him in Placerville one time." "Why, I seen *him* around town, *he* the Comanche?" Someone was playing a comb wrapped in paper, stopping at regular intervals to sing in a nasal voice:

> **Co-man-che, came to I-de-ho**
> **With a pal named Injun Pete**
> **A very shady character**
> **Who had broke from jail in Pike.**
> **But Ike got drunk in Lewiston**
> **And ended up in jail,**
> **And they hung him to a cottonwood**
> **Ere John could go his bail.**

"We'll write the last verse of that doggerel tonight!" a man whooped.

"There he comes!" Those on the street were shouting. "They're bringing the killer now."

"Don't give him a trial! Give him the same chance he gave the boys at Whiskey Gulch. Hang him now!"

Someone swung a blow at John as he passed. He weaved,

and the blow knocked his hat off. He could not pick it up. His hat was trampled. Someone else picked it up and stuck it back on his head.

"Keep away from the prisoner!" Finch was shouting. "He'll get a fair trial before we hang him. I'll kill any man tries to take my prisoner away from me."

"What you got to say for yourself, killing honest men from ambush?" a tall man shouted in his ear as he passed.

John answered: "I say killing them was a typical Yankee trick and I'm for Jeff Davis! I say I waren't even in the country when that was done and give me a day or two and I can prove it!"

"Listen to him! He wants a day or two! We're supposed to feed him at public expense for two days while he proves he ain't where he was."

Some pitch torches burned brightly with large volumes of smoke before the log building that served as a claim recorder's office, judge's office, and jail. He was taken toward it, carried in the sweep of the crowd. Newly sworn deputies were posted to keep clear the steps in front of the jail.

Judge Harrison, smelling of freshly consumed liquor, met them grandly with a law book under his right arm.

"Hold it outside!" everyone started to shout, and he acceded to the demand, telling two of the deputies to carry his table to the walk.

The platform was a couple feet off the ground and once there a man could breathe. A barrel of rain water stood near the door and John was tempted to dip his head into it, but, if he did, it would be like somebody to hold him under. Besides, the water gave him an idea. It was such an idea that made him want to whoop in glee, but he did not. He stood and looked like a condemned man should look. If only he could get himself close to the barrel, and if only it was full enough!

139

Judge Harrison clubbed the table with a gavel. He did not call a jury. He remarked in a loud voice there was just time before the trial for the spectators to repair to their favorite bar for a drink of Old Stonehouse bourbon and started calling the names of witnesses.

He swore in everyone who happened to raise his hand, saying the familiar sentence all in one breath, and then said: "Hoss Noon, take the stand."

Hoss stood and testified that John, when arrested, had two pokes of gold marked with the burned-in initials I.J.R. The two pokes were displayed. They were two of the pokes he had seen in Malloy's strongbox. They were identified as genuine. The gold was identified as the type found in Whiskey Gulch. The guns were shown to be .36 caliber like those used in the ambush and, for that matter, like two-thirds of the pistols in camp.

"Evidence conclusive!" shouted Harrison. He banged the table with his gavel. "Prisoner guilty. By the power vested in me by the territorial legislature and his honor, the governor, all duly elected by the citizens of this territory, I sentence the prisoner to hang by the neck until he is dead. Move out o' the way over there so the boys can get the freight wagon up to the mercantile platform, use it for a drop. We'll hang him off the jut end of the awning."

"Hold on," said John, "can't I speak in my own behalf? What kind of court of law ye running here?"

"Prisoner guilty, no sense in taking up the time of the court." The judge waved a stubby hand at the gold and John's brace of Navies. "Somebody carry these inside and provide for their safekeeping until such time as proper heirs and assigns have been established. Boy, will you run down to the Montana and fetch me a pint of Old Stonehouse bourbon, the pride of all Kentucky bourbons aged in the wood!"

As a sideline Judge Harrison was agent for the distillery and never missed an opportunity for advertising his product.

"Dang ye!" cried John, "right here in my pocket I can prove it's illegal to hang me. I can prove I was already hung over in I-de-ho City. Haven't ye ever heered of double jeprody? What kind of lawyer do ye call yourself anyhow?"

"Prisoner be quiet. Court will fine prisoner for contempt."

"What more can ye do to me than hang me?"

"Hang you with a rough rope. Lead this prisoner away."

"It ain't easy on a man, being hung," John said, changing his tone to one of sadness. "Even for a man like me, road agent, gunman wicked to shame Gomorrah. No, it ain't. Ain't easy going to face your maker with sin on your soul and your lump of righteousness nigh run empty. And I got dear ones at home. I don't guess you men of New Boston would want to swing a man without him having a fitten time to pray, and to write to his loved ones."

"Give him time!" some of them started to shout, but others were up angrily demanding: "How much time did he give the boys in Whiskey Gulch?"

"Gents, all I ask is a minister to help me pray and I'll hang with your praise on my lips."

Harrison, judging the temper of the crowd, said: "Compromise. Give you half an hour. Don't think we'll have the scaffold all fixed up much short of that anyhow. Boy, boy, where's my Old Stonehouse bourbon, the queen of Kentucky whiskies, aged ten long years in the wood?"

Malloy came through from the office and said: "What the devil! Get that man hanged."

"Not the will of the sovereign majority," said Judge Harrison.

"Well, keep watch of him. I don't trust some of these deputies of yours."

"What happened to Frenchy, Oregon, Step-And-A-Half, and them?"

"I told you. I need them out at the White Pine."

"You don't waste time!"

"I don't believe in wasting time. This is the ideal moment. Everyone is here. A little shooting out there will never be noticed." He dropped to the ground, and climbed to the high platform of the Territorial Mercantile Company next door where two men were arguing about placing the hang rope. Things speeded under Malloy's direction. The crowd was parted and a freight wagon with its end gate down was backed around beneath a projecting timber of the pole awning. A rope was tossed over the timber and Malloy with nimble fingers wrapped a hangman's knot in the end. "Pull it up!" he said, and they did, leaving the knot swinging with its grim loop in the torches.

It was evident they intended to stand their man on the wagon and hang him merely by driving it forward. Several in the crowd, old California men, objected, saying he would not be given a good drop.

"I believe in hanging," one of the California men kept saying over and over, "but I believe in giving 'em a good drop."

Malloy decided to move the wagon farther out and place a plank between the wagon box and the store platform. As before the drop would be released by driving the wagon forward, but the plank would allow the condemned man a straight fall.

"Good idee!" said the California man. "Never swing 'em, drop 'em. I say you can tell if a camp is first class by the way they stage their hangings."

John said—"I be mighty weary."—and edged to the rain barrel.

"Fifteen minutes gone," someone said. "We'll hang him whenever the scaffold's fixed."

"Well, she's nigh fixed."

Seeing John edge by the rain barrel, Huckven shouted: "Stay whar you are!"

"I'm tired. Surely ye can't deny a dying man the support of leaning on a bar'l."

"Skeered he'll git away from you?" someone taunted Huckven.

"No, I'm not skeered. I wish he'd try. I just wish it."

It had been a wet summer. There had been no nearby fires. The barrel was almost full. It was cool against his back. He tried to get his hands over the edge, but the rawhide wrappings were too tight. He got on tiptoe, he scissored his way up the barrel as if trying to sit on the edge. Huckven was watching, but John's back and hands were in shadow, and he did not realize that John had worked them over the edge of the barrel and that now they were plunged deep in the cool, stale water.

The rawhide was still tight, but its hard edge quickly softened. It became slick against his wrists. He kept working his arms and hands with a steady back and forth movement, feeling the rawhide loosen as it grew wet.

"Bring the prisoner," said Malloy.

"Half an hour!" shouted John. "I got twenty minutes yet."

"Your half hour started in the Montana House."

A man from the crowd shouted: "It started when you bushwhacked those poor boys over in Whiskey Gulch!"

Then a familiar voice came from across the heads of the crowd. "Lemme through, lemme through, brothers! Make way for a preacher on a sad errand. Don't stand in the way of a minister on his way to comfort the dying. Thankee, thankee."

It was the parson. Malloy saw him and cursed. Huckven lifted his Navy and aimed it at the parson's gray head, and Malloy barked: "Don't, you damn' fool!"

"This the man, this the poor condemned man?" the parson said, pointing to Comanche John. "The black-whiskered one? Repent ye! Are ye ready to depart? Please, gents, your favor! Let me be alone with this poor condemned man only a minute. I'll be personally responsible for his conduct. Let me take him inside."

"You can be alone with him out here!" Malloy said, pointing to the plank.

The parson was close then, and John said from the side of his mouth: "Don't you worry about me. They'll put no rope on my neck. You git to the valley. Git, and git fast, this is the hour Malloy has chosen to run ye out of your homes."

"John, you'll never get away. This is your finish. You've spit in the catamount's eye once too often, and *this* time you're bound to git clawed."

"Mebby, but I'll claw right back." He kept twisting his hands. The rawhide was far stretched now. He worked the bindings until they were all in one mass, and looser than ever. He could have slipped his hands out, but he didn't. He let them stay. He moved his hands from the barrel. He pressed them tightly against his back, getting the water off.

"Pray for me, Parson, don't make 'em suspicious."

The parson prayed as minutes passed and the crowd became impatient. At last the deputies pushed him out of the way.

"Git!" said John to him. "Saddle and ride. Fight 'em off. Give 'em a bellyful of lead and I'll wager before the sun sets tomorrow I'll get that grant to ye. I won't promise, but I'll wager it!"

Men gathered on both sides of Comanche John and led

him from the jail platform, to the ground, and up four steps to the platform of the Mercantile. He walked to the plank, and there they left him. He stood on the plank, hands behind him, testing its spring.

"Man might fall offen here," he said. "Thing like this could be dangerous."

Someone in the crowd whooped: "You'll fall off, but you'll never hit the ground!"

John made a last survey of the scene. He located the door to the judge's office. His Navies were inside on the table. He judged the distance from the plank to the ground, his best route beneath the platform. The chief portion of the crowd would stampede when the shooting commenced, and that would help. Everything was ready.

Then with a casual shift of his feet he stepped on the edge of the plank, and it flipped over, sending him to the ground.

He pulled his hands free of the rawhide and dived head foremost beneath the platform. Frightened by the sudden movement and the falling plank, the team bolted. The crowd went scattering. The driver was dragged by the reins, boot heels in the ground.

On hands and feet, traveling with the speed and agility of a baboon, John bounded through the pilings and braces. He came briefly into the open not five feet from Huckven, but in the milling crowd nobody saw him. He might have escaped between the store and the jail, but he wanted his Navies.

He crossed the platform, ducked through the door, grabbed up his Navies, and almost ran into Judge Harrison who was coming from the rear of the building to see what the excitement was.

The judge stopped, mouth agape, making no sound.

"Tonight," said John, ramming one of the Navies in the judge's stomach, "ye will see invoked a portion of the law never gone into much by Blackstone. This here is called the Colt statchoot, she's got six sections, and they's no appeal from any of 'em. Now, maybe, I'll invoke it, and maybe I won't. It depends on whether you're more alive or dead. So do what I say. Pick up the candle. Walk and keep me in the shadow. Be blamed sure I'm in the shadow!"

The room was lighted by three candles in a reflecting holder. Holding this light ahead of him, the judge did as John commanded. He paused at the door with John right behind him.

"We'll go yonder," John said. "To the left, tight ag'in' the building. If I'm lucky, and *you're* lucky, nobody'll see us at all."

But a man sang out: "Huckven! Look there, behind the judge!"

Judge Harrison, his muscles solidified by fear, had stopped in the wrong place. Comanche John tripped him and rammed him sprawling from the platform. It left John in the clear then for three running strides. A gun exploded so close he could feel the burn of powder and the wind of passing lead against the back of his neck. He turned. He saw Huckven with smoking gun in his hands swinging for another shot. He fired with his left-hand Navy and the bullet doubled the tall Huckven in the middle as though he'd been struck by a club. Huckven staggered forward and recovered enough to fire both pistols wildly as a second slug hit him and spun him, wrapping one leg around the other and dropping on his back with his arms out.

"Thar ye been looking for it!" John whooped. He made a long leap from the platform as bullets from four different directions tore splinters from the corner of the building.

He answered with a stream of lead from both Navies. The street was a wild, shoving, cursing stampede for cover.

John ducked behind the platform walk of the jail. Crabwise he got himself back in the narrow passage between the jail and a Chinese hand laundry. Bullets came in volleys. A bullet ripped along the wall, carving splinters that stung his face and showered his pulled-down hat.

"Whar are ye, Walker Malloy?" he whooped. "Come out, bring your deputies, tell 'em it's suppertime and I'm serving red-hot biscuits, every one guaranteed to last a lifetime."

Missou was coming belly down beneath the platform. John saw and drove him back with one ear and half the brim of his hat shot away.

"Ya-hoo!" shouted Comanche John, kicking dust with his jackboots, "ye know who I be? Waal, listen and I'll tell ye. I'm Comanche John from Yuba Gulch. I was born in Pike County, Missouri and raised on catfish and corn likker. I pick my teeth with the cactus bush and drink water out of the crick like a horse. Last winter I craved raw meat and was plumb out o' bullets so I lit in to a grizzly bar with my teeth. Now, if ye should see a three-legged grizzly, give him room because he detests the sight o' man. Waal, I crave raw meat tonight, and I ain't seen a grizzly in two, three weeks, so clear out o' my way and give me room because I'm shootin' mad with my Navy guns."

X

"SHARE AND SHARE ALIKE"

He retreated between the buildings, firing his guns empty. There was darkness and the rising steepness of the gulch at the rear. Ambush in that direction. He found a side door to the hand laundry. He went inside, met by damp heat and laundry smells. Someone in the dark was babbling Chinese.

"Ho, thar!" said John. "I'm short of lead tonight and don't figure on shooting no Chineemen. Git me out o' hyar. Come on, damn ye, or don't ye speak human?"

There were Chinese on all sides of him now, all chattering. One of them opened a rear door. He could see the gray of approaching dawn through it. The area behind the laundry was full of movement. Malloy was shouting orders in one direction, Finch in another. He stopped for a moment of indecision and thought of the roof. He ran from one end of the laundry to the other cursing under his breath. "Every place has a fire hole. Even a Chinee place should have a fire hole."

He located some wooden cleats pegged to the wall. He climbed. They led through a lid door to the roof. He pushed it aside, emerged into the open. The roof was wide and flat. He ran, crouched over; he leaped the intervening five or six feet to the gable roof of the saloon next door. He climbed over the ridge, slid down the far side, slowing his descent by digging in the nails of his boot heels. He dropped to earth without breaking a leg and stood against the wall breathing and taking a quick look front and back. He decided to return to the street. Men were on the run trying to get in on the fight or escape from it. In the general flux no one paid the slightest heed to him. He walked. He reloaded his Navies while he walked. The crowd had thinned out. He was all by himself, walking. A young man carrying a Navy in his hand came on the run and rammed into him. The fellow rebounded against the front of a saloon and became popeyed when he saw who John was.

"Yep," John said, a Navy aimed at his middle, "it's me, the Comanche, and ye lived to tell the tale. Now, I'll just take your Navy to keep ye out of trouble."

He took it and walked on with the young man gaping at him, too stunned and trembling to say a word. He entered a dark side street. He ran. He climbed a zigzag trail up the gulch. He circled a cluster of small buildings and doubled back to the rear of the Montana House. The doors were all open; there was not a soul in the place. He dumped over card tables, tossed chairs in a heap, found the store of camphene for the stage lights. Camphene was a mixture of turpentine and alcohol and almost explosive as gunpowder. "Why, this was like for the purpose," John said, drenching the heap with it and adding a keg of whale oil for good measure. He tossed a lighted candle in and watched the flame take hold and spread. Then he went out the back and waited, chewing and getting his breath, giving a satisfied ear to the roaring progress of the fire.

"Fire! Fire!" Foolish Mike Peabody was shouting, booming his bass drum. "Fire in the Montana House, pray for rain!"

149

Already smoke was rolling through open doors and windows. In the distance came the *clang-clang* of the new pumping wagon. Soon the volunteer fire laddies had the intake end of their hose in the muddy sluice-tail discharge of the gulch, playing a stream inside, producing great volumes of steam while in no way halting the spread of the flames.

"Save the likker!" men were shouting. "To hell with that piano, save the likker!"

Two men came on the run through the back alleyway—Malloy and Max the Ape. They passed John so closely he could have hit them with tobacco juice, and up the stairs they charged two steps at a time.

"Working out fine," said John. "Working like a Swisslander clock. It's like I told the parson, what ye need is a man with brains. Man that'll figure things out, judge human nature. Want to make a man do the right thing all ye got to do is make him itch in the right place. Now Malloy has got a thing to save and a thing to hide. He'll walk into my arms and all I need is to be ready for him."

He checked his Navies and put them back in their holsters. He sauntered to the stairway. He yawned, scratched his whiskers, and looked around at the dawn, thinking it would be better if it were not so light, and better still if he had a horse ready. But his horse was yonder in the corral, and folks hereabouts still had plenty of diversion.

Then he heard Malloy and the ape at the head of the stairs; they were struggling with the heavy strongbox.

"Put it down, we'll slide it," Malloy said.

They did, letting it *thud-thud* down the steps, the ape below checking its descent, Malloy tugging it by a handle above.

At the bottom they let it sit while straightening to rest their backs, and at that second Malloy saw John.

"Yep," said John, slouching toward them, "it be me. I run, but I didn't run far. Just far enough to start that bonfire, wait out behind knowing ye'd bring it . . . the gold sponge, the gold from Whiskey Gulch, and that paper, the fur company grant ye talked poor Wally Snite into stealing, and then kilt him in payment. Thought you'd want to share it. Share and share alike's my motto."

John had not drawn his Navies. His hands were nowhere near his Navies. He stood scratching the side of his neck with his right hand and a place under his ribs with his left. He was chewing and he turned to spit, and Malloy, with a sudden, bitter laugh, saw what he thought was his chance and with a leap and quarter whirl went for the pearl-handled gun at his waist.

He was fast, faster than John had expected, and in moving he had placed himself partially behind the broad form of the ape, but John, with a forward slouch and a straightening of his body, beat him to the draw. He seemed almost casual about it, yet the guns were there in his hands and the backward tilt of his body had pointed them. They exploded. One of the bullets hit Malloy in the region of his left shoulder. It was not a fatal wound, but the shock of lead sent him reeling and off balance. He fired one shot into the ground. He turned, his gun making a silvery gleam in the dawn. He fired once again just as two slugs from John's Navies hit him with a coupled impact that knocked him flat in the dust.

The ape had meantime dived for cover. He got in one wild shot and no more.

Then it was all over, and John stood over them, looking at them through the smoke of his guns. "Why, this is what I should have done in the first place. *Would* have, too, only that dratted parson talked me out of it."

The parchment had not been inside the strongbox and

probably it was not there now. He had a hunch, and it proved a good one. He found it the first grab, inside the breast pocket of Malloy's coat.

"Leave it like this," he said. "Stolen gold, Malloy's strongbox, Malloy beside it. Even a pack of Union Abolitionists ought to see the guilty one *now*. Waal, it's no never mind for me. I've sickened of this place. Too many houses, too many people. By grab, the country's getting too damn' civilized. Next thing those farmers out on the bottoms will be plowing and planting and you won't be able to tell Montana from Ioway. It's the north country for me, the Blackfeet country, Canady even."

He went to the livery stable, found everyone gone, watching the fire. He saddled his gunpowder horse and rode upgulch and over the hills. In the distance toward the White Pine was gunfire, a few shots separated by minutes of quiet. The sun rose and shone hot and good on his back, making him shed his buckskin jacket. He sat, letting his horse graze, and had a long view of the valley. None of the buildings had been burned, everything seemed peaceful, but the guns kept popping intermittently. He rode, following the sound and saw where Overfelt, Noon, Step-And-A-Half and that bunch were holed up among some boulders at the near edge of the valley while the farmers were smoking them from two sides.

It was a fair fight, and he enjoyed it. He considered stirring up the "deputies" from the rear and decided against it. "Had *my* fun," he said. "No use of intruding in on *their* fun. No use to be hoggish. Let 'em have the satisfaction of saving their homes for themselves. Besides, if I went thar and made a hero of myself, I'd likely be drug off to be feasted by that Cobb woman. She'd git me at my comfort, feet up, in a rocking chair, full of her stew and fritters, can't tell what I'd do. Marry her even."

He rode, avoiding the houses. From a distance he hailed the Shallerbach kid who was sentry against surprise attack. He gave him the parchment, told him to deliver it to the parson, and asked concerning the events of the night before. The parson, young Shallerbach said, had busted in at a gallop and warned them just in time. "We met 'em with smoking lead!" the kid said. "Teach them a lesson about claim jumping. What's this paper, anyhow?"

"You give it to the parson, *he'll* know what it is."

He rode on, crossed White Pine Creek deep as the gunpowder's belly, and rode up a winding draw that split the hills to the north. He could no longer hear any shooting. He kept the horse at a jog. He rode with his black slouch hat on the back of his head favoring the spot where Malloy had slugged him the night before. He seemed sleepy, but his eyes had a wary habit, watching as the country opened in new vistas with each turn in the draw. Sometimes he sang, his voice a tuneless monotone, the words bumped from him by the movements of the horse:

Waal, I hail from old Missouri
Up in the County Pike,
And whenever I draw m'Navies out
It's share and share alike!

Salvation Guns

I

The black-whiskered man had been riding for a long time. Fatigue was evident in his slouched posture as he kept the gunpowder roan ambling along the cutbank rim, watching the Yellowstone River that glistened pleasantly in evening's last light below. Finally he drew up. It was apparent he'd seen the thing he had been looking for—a pinpoint of light marking the camp of a river brigade.

He didn't immediately ride down. He sat for a while, one knee crooked over the horn of his Spanish saddle, and watched. He was about forty, shorter and broader than most men. His face, where it could be seen around its tangle of black whiskers, had been weathered the hue of old leather. He wore a buckskin shirt, trousers of gray homespun, dusty jackboots, no spurs. An ancient slouch hat sat on his head. Around his waist, sagging naturally from long habit, were two Navy Colts.

The roan cayuse cropped August-dry buffalo grass for a while, then, still taking his time, the black-whiskered man put him down a crooked cutbank trail, and cut across the two or three miles of river bottom to pause, half hidden by sagebrush and box elder trees to watch.

There was a fire burned down to coals and a freckled kid,

tall as a man, sitting beside it, twanging a banjo. Beyond, by the ruddy light, he could see two big, awkward bullboats drawn ashore and tilted with their hide bottoms toward the fire to dry. The roof of a willow lean-to was visible to the right.

The kid found banjo chords that pleased him, and sang:

> **Co-man-che John was a highwayman**
> **Who hailed from County Pike,**
> **He had a pal named Larry-bee**
> **And one called Injun Ike,**
> **Three faster shootin' curly wolves**
> **You seldom ever knew.**
> **Oh! listen to my storee,**
> **I'll tell ye what they do:**
> **They ride to Oro-Fino**
> **On the old Snake River trail**
> **To rob the coach at Pistol Rock**
> **And stop the Western mail. . . .**

The lad sang with measured mournfulness, playing solo passages on the banjo, and three stanzas took him at least five minutes. The whiskered man heard him to the end, chewing in rhythm with the banjo, then he rode on into the firelight, drawing up, reaching for the ground with a dusty jackboot.

The lad jerked around, jolted by so quiet an approach, and sat with his jaw sagging, watching as the whiskered one ambled forward on stiffened legs.

"Who are you?" he managed to gulp.

"I don't reckon that's a polite question in this Nor'west country, son." The whiskered man paused to aim at a quartz pebble and splatter it with a spurt of tobacco juice. "Never ask a man whar he's headed or what his name is. He might be

155

somebody like that Comanche John woolly-wolf you was singing about and take offense. But me . . . I'm peaceful as a Chinee on Saint Patrick's day. I ain't got nothing but Christian brotherhood in my heart for nobody."

The kid's eyes had shifted to something back in the dark, and the whiskered man noticed, sagging a trifle to the right side, making the butt of that Navy six swing out a little, but, if he had an idea of drawing, he changed his mind when a saw-edged voice cut the night.

"Keep your hands clear, stranger."

"Why, sure. I got the most innocent hands between here and Ioway. Do ye mind if I turn around?"

"Suit yourself."

He turned slowly, careful to make no abrupt movement that might be misinterpreted, his jaw still revolving thoughtfully around the cud of blackjack tobacco. He could see him then, a long, loose-jointed man holding a rifle waist high.

"Who in hell are you?" the tall man asked.

"You see, son? This tall gent understands how things should be done. Iffen you want to know a man's handle, first off you point a gun at him."

The tall one barked: "I'm in no mood to take any o' your lip."

"Why, then, I'll just have to own up to being named Smith. John Smith."

"What you here for?"

"I been ridin' considerable. Clear from the Sulphur Bottoms, and nothing but chawing tobacco in between. So, seeing your camp. . . ."

"Anybody with you?"

"Just me and my cayuse."

He grunted and lowered the rifle. Not all the way, but he lowered it. "We ain't cravin' company."

"White men in this country generally. . . ."

"We ain't cravin' company!" he barked more loudly. "Not with every odd man a road agent and the in-between ones worse. You better get your rump on that saddle, stranger, and shake a bush."

"The parson hereabouts?"

The question made the tall man straighten and his eyeballs look more pointed than ever. "Who?"

"The Reverend Parker, known from here to Feather River as the parson. I be a friend o' his."

"He ain't. . . ."

The freckled kid broke in: "He's downriver, helpin' bring in some meat."

"Red, keep your flappin' tongue tied down or I'll wrap this rifle bar'l around your magpie neck."

Red stood his ground. "I only. . . ."

"I heered what you said. . . ."

A woman's voice came from the direction of the river. "What the thunderation's goin' on up thar?"

She charged into sight, gaunt, huge, and raw-boned, an Eight-Gauge double-gun in her hands. She swung it around so the barrel was angled at the tall man's feet.

"Shepherd, I told you before not to pick on Red. I ain't goin' to stand for it, d'you hear?"

"Damn it, Mast left me here to. . . ."

"Watch your language in front of a woman or you'll find yourself pickin' bird shot out o' your hindquarters clean from here to Fort Union." She turned then and glowered at the whiskered man. "And who be you?"

The man's black whiskers parted in a grin. "I'm hungry."

The woman leaned her Eight Gauge against a supply box and snorted. "Now that's a nach'rel man answer if I ever heard one. 'Who be you?' I ask. 'I'm hungry,' says he. Well, the Lord put man varmints in the world to lay around and eat grub, and I reckon he put womenfolks here to cook victuals and feed 'em." She wheeled and bellowed into the downriver darkness. "It's all right, Jennie. It's just a whiskered he-wolf with an empty stomach. You carry up that stew and we'll feed him."

A girl walked into sight, biting her lower lip from the effort as she carried a big iron kettle. She was slim, dark-haired, pretty.

Her body, molded by the calico dress, was just swelling into womanhood. Red watched her in a breathless way for a while, then he hopped to his feet and helped her set the kettle on the coals.

The whiskered man watered and unsaddled his gun-powder roan. When he came back after picketing the animal in a fat stand of buffalo grass, the stew was *thump-thumping* in the kettle. The woman ladled up a tin plate of it—buffalo, wild turnips, and dumplings.

"I'm Prudence Boomer," she rumbled. "And comin' yonder is Cyrus, my man." She jerked her head at a blunt-faced fellow, as big as she was, who came, sleepy-eyed, from the lean-to.

Cyrus Boomer said: "Reckon Shep yonder didn't mean to be rough on you, stranger, but a man's got to keep his gun primed what with the road agents crowdin' the trails from Virginia City now that the vigilance committee is fitten 'em with Californy collars."

"Well, share and share alike is my motto," the whiskered man said, sitting cross-legged, plate on his knees, and stabbing buffalo meat with his Bowie knife. "And that's scripture right out of 'Zekiel, verse six."

"Amen!" whooped Prudence Boomer. "It's good to associate with a Christian for a change. Boomer, yonder, ain't got no more religion than a swamp hawg. You read the Bible much, whiskers?"

"I read 'er from Ab to Abbernathy and back to Beer-sheba." He rammed buffalo meat in his mouth and talked around it. "Shacked up with a real sure enough reverend over at Yankee Bar. Handle of Reverend Parker."

"Parker? An ornery old rooster with a skinny neck?"

"Best description of him I ever heard."

"He's here! With this bullboat outfit. Only right now he went downriver to help haul buffalo meat on the travois drag."

"Amen and hallelujah!"

He finished the plateful, and stowed away two more, telling of the times he stood shoulder to shoulder with the parson fighting the devil and his earthly cohorts. "He blasted 'em with scripture, and I leaned a bit toward doing the job with a Navy six, but I reckon it takes a bit o' one with the other, the Nor'west being what it is."

That said, he leaned back, picking his teeth with the Bowie. He seemed sleepy and off guard, but his eyes remained alive, keeping watch on the camp between slitted lids.

The bullboats were the kind fur traders used to transport cargo downstream during low water. They were wide, ugly, and awkward. Untanned buffalo hides sewn together with babiche, stretched over frames of birch, the seams calked with a mixture of wood ashes and tallow. They had been hoisted ashore and tilted with their bottoms toward the fire, for such craft, while light enough to clear the sandbars of late summer, had the disadvantage of becoming water-logged after a day of travel.

Stacked along the bank nearby were some buffalo hides pressed and tied in bales, but, despite the cargo and means of travel, these people were obviously not fur traders. They were

Pike's Peakers, emigrants from Missouri who had turned north from the Oregon Trail to join the rush to the gold camps of Montana, and now they were headed back. The cargo was obviously a blind.

"More of your boys upstream?" he asked Red.

The lad was hunkered, twanging his banjo. He nodded, keeping his voice low, his eyes on Shep who was prowling around, hawk-faced with suspicion. "Dunny Schmidt . . . he's asleep under number one boat. Rest of 'em are downstream, dragging meat with the travois. Elvis Mast and the rest."

There was a certain way that he spoke that name, Elvis Mast.

"Who's he . . . your leader?"

He gave the banjo a vicious twang. "Thinks he is!"

"And Shep, yonder. Does he think Mast is boss, too?"

"Yep."

"But Prudence Boomer . . . I'll lay Confederate gold to Union greenbacks she won't admit no boss here excepting herself."

Red twisted his skinny face out of joint grinning and let it go at that.

The whiskered man sighed and stretched his jackboots a few inches farther. "You was singing a mighty purty song when I rode up. About a varmint coach robber by the handle of Comanche John. Wonder if you've learnt a verse that goes like this," and he started singing in a tuneless monotone:

Co-man-che John came to Yallerjack
In the year of 'Sixty-Three
To rob the stage at Hoss Crick
And the sluice at Lone Teepee. . . .

He broke off abruptly, turning with an agility one would

not have expected of him, and hunkered on the heels of his scuffed jackboots in the shadow of the upended bullboat; his hands were down, fingers lightly on the legs of his homespuns just beneath the holstered Navies.

Red had obviously heard nothing. For the space of ten or twelve seconds there was no sound, only the little contraction sounds of embers turning themselves into ash. Then, from a distance across the river bottoms, came a *click* of hoof on stone.

"Where'd the pilgrim go?" Prudence asked, coming up from the river with a bucket of water to settle for breakfast.

"I'm here." His voice came from shadow. "And as far as you're concerned, you never seen me. I made me some enemies here and there, helping that wooden-headed parson bust up sin."

She was suspicious, bent over, peering beyond the bullboat. Then, not answering, she stepped back from the firelight and tried to see through night and box elder bramble where hoofs were thudding and bridle chains jingled. In a couple of minutes four men rode into the light.

One of them, a short, powerful man, swung down and walked over on horse-stiffened legs. The other three sat back, watching, alert.

"Hello, over there!" he called in a raw, weary voice, peering at Red. Red got up, laying aside his banjo. His face, being nervous, looked longer than ever. "What sort o' camp is this?"

"Bullboat camp," said Prudence, crossing toward him. "What you lookin' for?"

"Wolves."

"There's been plenty of 'em howlin' back yonder in the breaks."

"We're lookin' for the two-legged kind."

"Maybe we got them, too." She was flat-faced and hostile, hands on hips, the shotgun leaning against a box of grub not too far away. "Any special wolf in particular?"

"A black-whiskered one, 'less he's shaved, which isn't likely. Renegade named Comanche John."

Red dropped the banjo. The short man's eyes knifed over and rested on him. They were the sort of eyes that seemed to penetrate beneath the surface.

"What's wrong, son? You seen him?"

"No. Leastwise. . . . No, I ain't. I was just singin' a song about him. That's all. When you rode up. . . ."

The man growled something. One of his companions, a lean, reddish-mustached man, climbed down with pants sticking to the insides of his legs from the sweat of long travel. "Look around, Rafe," the short one said to him.

He turned back to Prudence Boomer: "I'm Lyn Creedle. Alder Gulch."

"Long way from home, ain't you?"

"We shook a few miles o' dust. Fetched ourselves a wolf over on Mason Ranch yesterday. Name of Windy Jim Price. Fitted him up with a new collar. A collar guaranteed to wear him for keeps."

"Was he a road agent?"

"Why, there's them that said he was, and them that said he wasn't. So, not wantin' to take any chances, we hung him."

"Whar I was brung up, back in Pike County, Missouri, we always believed in makin' pretty sure of a man before. . . ."

"It's a long shake over the hill to Pike County, ma'am."

"Why, so it be. But I dare say you're sure this Comanche John. . . ."

"They run him out of Yuba City, and they run him out of Detman Bar, and Yallerjacket. But we ain't runnin' him out of Montana country. We'll catch him by sundown tomorrow, and fix him up so he'll stick around, permanent."

"I ain't seen him!" Cyrus Boomer had just plodded up, and his wife turned on him. "Cy, these gents is Alder Gulch stranglers and they're aimin' to fetch a lone wolf by the name of Comanche John . . . and we ain't seen him."

Boomer didn't say anything. He merely stood with his boots set wide, looking uneasy.

The vigilante said: "Mind if we search the camp?"

"You seem to be a-doing it."

He turned and for the first time noticed Shep Shepherd. Shepherd had his back up against a tangle of rose thorns, watching with protruding, close-set eyes.

Creedle asked: "You see a black-whiskered stranger hereabout?"

"They ain't be a stranger here tonight," Shepherd said, his voice loud and high-pitched. "Just our own bunch."

After a while one of the horsemen rode in, leading the gunpowder roan by his plaited, rawhide rope.

"Gone a long way since morning." Creedle squinted at the animal's tracks. "Whose horse?"

Boomer took a deep breath, but Prudence rammed him, making him stop.

"He's mine," said Red. "I rode him scoutin' for Blackfeet."

His voice had been steady enough, and from their distance none of the vigilantes noticed the glisten of perspiration on his upper lip.

Creedle barked: "That's a Mormon mark on his hip. Where'd you buy him?"

"Fort Hall."

"Who from?"

"Fellow with a remount pasture."

"What was his name?"

Red hesitated a while. "Generoux."

"I don't know any Generoux at Fort Hall."

Red was scared almost to tears. "There is too. . . ."

"There's a Frenchy at Fort Hall, right enough," one of the vigilantes said. "Picks up fallen ones from the Oregon Trail and pastures 'em. Let's get to movin'."

Creedle tossed the picket rope toward Red, then he took time to sniff the air. "Ain't that victuals I smell?"

Prudence growled: "Only thing I smell hereabouts is skunk."

He laughed, brittle, the way a man laughs when he's tired. "What's wrong, lady? Don't you like havin' the country made safe for you?" He swung back to the saddle. "Sorry to turn your grub down, but we'll have to drift if we're to make Rambeau Crossing by sunup. He'll be headin' there. Comanche John. If you like, we'll leave him swingin' there so you can see what a *good* road agent looks like!"

II

No one spoke for almost a minute after the four vigilantes had disappeared in box elder brush. Then the black-whiskered man edged back in range of the fire and hunkered, still keeping the bushes between himself and the flats.

"You can breathe now, Shep." He grinned.

Shep relaxed and filled his lungs. "You sure enough Comanche John?"

"That's one o' the names I been called."

Words rushed from Shep's lips now that fear had left him. "You didn't have to toss those Navies at me, John. I wouldn't't've turned you over to them stranglers. I ain't got no love for. . . ."

"Never mind."

Prudence Boomer was glaring. "You! A Christian! And here you're nothin' but a pistol-shootin', no-account, tobacco-chewin' road agent that. . . ."

"Hold on. I own to being all them things except road agent. Not since the parson fetched me religion. Since then, I been innocent as a babe unborn. Share and share alike, that's my motto."

"We'll see soon enough if you're the parson's friend or not."

★ ★ ★ ★ ★

The parson and half a dozen others arrived a while later, weary and dusty, using cordelle lines to help two cayuse horses drag travois heavy with hump and leg meat from three cow buffalos.

"Hallelujah!" bellowed Comanche John, kicking up dust in a war dance when he sighted the parson. "How's business with the sinners?"

"Comanche John! You old. . . ." He stopped himself abruptly. "I suppose you're here, on the lope as usual, with a posse after you for some deviltry. . . ."

"I been up to no deviltry, Parson!" John roared, beating dust from the old man's woolsey jacket. "I been treading the thorny trail o' rectitude no matter what them lying muleskinners wrote into that song o' theirs about me."

"So they didn't hang ye in Virginny City, after all. I heered they'd hung twenty-two of the worst in the territory, so natchilly I supposed you was one of 'em." The parson let his face become as sanctimonious as a hungry buzzard's. "I prayed for ye, John. Right down on these bony old knees, I prayed for ye. Many's the time. Amid cactus and cockleburs, alkali and dump quartz. I prayed for ye, John, even though I know it's blamed near useless, because premonition tells me that one o' these days you're goin' to git hung."

John spat. "They'll ride down some long coulées before they get one o' their hemp cravats around this neck." He linked the parson's arm, swinging him around for a word in private. "What sort of a dang' fool brigade do ye call this? You trying to float clean through Blackfoot country?"

"We'll take care of any Blackfeet."

"Hell, if I'd been a Blackfoot tonight, I'd have scalped ye all. Looks to me like you was headed for Saint Louis with a cargo of gold. You'll never make it, Parson. They're fixing to

166

ambush you. The Bloods. I seen 'em downriver and hunted this camp out special to warn ye off. Take my advice and sink these leaky hide-boats. Head cross-country to the Bozeman Trail. There's a blacksmith at Lone Tree fixes abandoned emigrant wagons, and you can buy an outfit. . . ."

A voice broke in behind him: "What you trying to do, split us up so we'll be cut down to a size you can handle?"

John turned slowly and peered at the man who was walking toward him. He was young, twenty-eight or thirty, lean and hard with the stamp of years along the fur and gold frontier. Six feet—a trifle more. Good-looking up as far as his eyes, but they spoiled it—pale and hard as twin fragments of broken gray quartz. He was dressed in buckskin, cut to fit his powerful limbs. Around his waist was a belt bearing one of those new .44-caliber Army revolvers and a long-bladed Green River knife. No powder horn. The revolver used metallic cartridges.

"You Elvis Mast?" John asked.

It flattered him a little to be known. "Yes. And you're Comanche John."

"I been called that handle some."

"What do you want?"

"The parson's an old friend o' mine."

Mast laughed, jerking his head back. "A preacher and a road agent. That's a hell of a combination." The laugh vanished from his face, leaving it cruel and hard-drawn. "Well, you've shaken hands. What are you waiting for?"

"You want me to pull my picket pin and drift?"

"Yes." He stood with hands on hips, corners of his mouth twisted down. He might have gone about it easier, only there was a circle of men around, listening. "Get out. Quick. Before somebody gets an idea with a rope. We don't like road agents here."

"Hold on, Mast!" The parson, in his wrath, got to hopping on his skinny legs. "You ain't got full say in this outfit. John can stay or git out, just as the boys decide. By majority. But first we better listen to what he's got to say."

Mast turned on the parson. He started forward, checked himself. His face had turned dark, muscles bulged, tightening the buckskin of his shirt, his fists knotted at the ends of his long arms. He trembled a little, trying to control himself.

"I agree with the parson," a red-faced man broke in. He had a good-humored voice that took some of the tension away. "He's got Providence on his side, and I say there's nothing a man needs in Blackfoot country like Providence."

"Sure, we'll hear him," a husky miner named Jackson said.

John chewed and spat. "Well, it's like this. The parson, yonder, is my shepherd, sort of, and, when I heered he was headed downriver, I reckoned I'd drop in and see him. So this evening I was ridge riding along, when what did I spy but gun shine and being curious for one reason or. . . ."

"Come to the point!" Mast barked.

"Why, so I be. As I said, I spied gun shine. Down yonder at what's called Brulé Point, on account of the Injun-burnt cabin there, Brulé meaning. . . ."

"What did you see?" Jackson asked.

"Why, Injuns. Fifteen or twenty. I left the gunpowder back in the draw and bellied up for a look-see. War party. Blackfeet. Blood branch o' the Blackfeet, by their shield marks. They was making war medicine, or I don't know Injun sign. Digging in behind willows, right where the current sets in. I'd hate to ride by in one o' these pesky bullboats come tomorrow."

The Pike's Peakers were silent and apprehensive, but Mast's face was gaunt and savage as before. He jerked his head and laughed.

168

"Quite a story. Only it's a lie."

John chewed the same as always. "Good to have backing when you call folks liars, ain't it?"

"Sure it's a lie!" Shep chimed in.

A French-Cree *voyageur* named Rechlin took his cue and added his voice: "Thees story! Pah! Ambush. Ain't we got scout? Bes' damn' Injun scout on prairee? If Blackfoot Stillman see not thees ambush, she's not there."

"We better have a look," Jackson growled.

Mast lifted a hand for silence. Then he addressed John: "All right. So you saw Injuns. What do you want us to do?"

"Like I just said to the parson, leave these bull-hide scows and go cross country to Lone Tree. You got horses to take your valuables, and you can foot it in two days. Get wagons and stock in Lone Tree and head for Fort Laramie, then downtrail to Leavenworth. You're taking gold dust to the States and have an idee of fooling road agents with that cargo of buffalo hides. Hell! . . . with the Injuns war-pathing from here to Mandan country you don't stand a chance."

Mast laughed again. He turned to the others. "He's not foolin' you, is he? He's a road agent. He wants to split us up. I dare say he has a gang out there. . . ."

Jackson said: "I'm stickin' by the boats, Injuns be damned, but all the same I'd like to take a look-see at Brulé before we name him a road agent and run him off."

"I said he gets out!" shouted Mast. "Do you hear me, Jackson? I organized this trip and I said he goes out."

Mast took a swaggering step forward, but Jackson was no coward. He stood his ground. "We been settling things by majority vote, Mast, even if you do own better'n half the gold. I say we vote on this, and, by grab, I'm not for runnin' the Comanche off if he's tellin' true about Brulé."

"What say you, Boomer?" another Pike's Peaker asked.

"I ain't favored toward a ruckus, and if this here road agent aims to come here. . . ."

"Boomer!" Prudence bellowed.

"All right, I vote to hold off till we have a look at Brulé." He glared at John. "But if we don't find Injuns. . . ."

Mast looked at them, jerked his shoulders in a brittle laugh. He didn't call for a vote. It was obvious how it would be. There'd be Shepherd, a keelboat man named Dunny Schmidt, the half-breed, and himself on one side, and all the Pike's Peakers on the other. Even if his scout, Blackfoot Stillman, rode in, he'd be a vote short.

John watched him narrowly and spat tobacco juice in the direction of his heels as he walked off. "Seems to me your friend Mast wants you to git in an Injun ambush," he said to the parson.

"No, John. He's bull-headed, and mean when he thinks he's right, but he ain't bushin' us. He's got more gold in that boat o' his than we got in ours, all of us put together. And that's aplenty. All these boys been workin' claims at Luckyshot Gulch. Thin gravel, pockety, and they worked it clean in one summer. Aimed to get out. Too risky through road-agent country to Salt Lake, so we decided to build a Mackinaw boat and float her out. Only we didn't have water enough for a Mackinaw. Mast joined up with us at Pipestone Creek. Hired Blackfoot for scout, Rechlin for a meat hunter, Dunny Schmidt as river man, and Shep for guard."

"Parson, there's somethin' wrong with this. I felt it when I rode in. You better change your mind and shake the dust with me. They's new gold strikes in Colorado that'll be drawing in the sinners like a faro game in hell. That's whar you be needed, Parson. Down thar, running a mission. Stick with this brigade, and that gray hair o' yours will end up on a Blackfoot medicine stick."

"Can't go, John. I had a hand in this, and I'm stickin' with 'em."

"Then there's nothing I can do but ride along with you and see if I can save your hide."

Mast was talking to the big-beaked half-breed, Rechlin. John was watching them. He left the parson, and walked toward them, a careless shuffle, arms swinging loosely at his sides. He knew Mast wasn't through. The man intended to follow it up—that night.

Mast saw him and turned. "I told you to get out. I meant it. I still mean it. Get out!"

"No. Reckon I'll stay. For tonight, anyhow. What you aim to do about it? Reach for that fancy pistol?" Then John shook his head and answered the question himself. "No. That ain't your style. You ain't the kind that figures on takin' a chance. Your kind figures on playing the sure thing."

He kept coming carelessly, jaw revolving around the tobacco. Without warning he spun, flung himself to one side. He'd expected a bullet in the back. There was none. Only surprised movement and a glimmer of gun shine. Shep swinging the rifle. The movement of John's hand was so smooth and practiced it was almost imperceptible, yet it brought the right-hand Navy from its holster. He fired, aiming across his body.

A sharp report, a streak of burning powder. The bullet struck with a ringing sound. Shepherd's rifle exploded at almost the same instant, but its bullet hit the earth, glanced, and whined past, almost striking the half-breed's knee.

Shepherd had dropped the gun and bent double, clutching his right wrist. Blood was running in a quick stream, dribbling from the tips of his fingers. The bullet had evidently struck somewhere between his hand and the rifle breech, and glanced, tearing the flesh of wrist and forearm.

Comanche John moved aside, still slouched, the Navy angled slightly up, a bit of powder smoke drifting from its muzzle.

He said: "It ain't often I give back-shooters a second chance, but this here's my night for doing a charitable deed."

Men shouted, crowded forward. Boomer's voice was loudest of anyone's. "Dammit! . . . ridin' in here, shootin' our men . . . !"

"Shut up, Paw. Neither of us seen what went on."

Mast's right hand was twitching along the leg of his buckskin trousers, but he made no move toward the .44 Colt. Instead, he turned and said to the Pike's Peakers: "I say that calls for rope."

Jackson looked over the scene and growled to the effect that Shep hadn't been hurt badly.

"Tried to kill him!" shouted Mast.

"You don't need to yell at me. I can hear without it."

John said: "I put that bullet right whar I intended. And next time he gets bushwhack idees, I'll put it right betwixt his eyes."

Shep was nether popular nor badly hurt, and the men were dusty and tired. Half an hour later all except the look-out had crawled into their blankets beneath the hide-boats.

III

Comanche John had spent a good many of his years sleeping "on the lope" with one eye open, so, when the scout, Blackfoot Stillman, rode in sometime during the timeless hours past midnight, he rolled over and watched through the bushes to see what he would do.

Blackfoot was a tall man, made to look taller by the little, gotch-eared pony he rode. He had the same tangled long hair and unkempt beard as when John saw him last. On his right hip was one of those big, double-barreled Texas pistols. A Hudson's Bay knife long as a man's forearm was sheathed at his belt, and he carried two egg-shaped powder horns, one on each side.

Mast came out to meet him. They walked away, shoulder to shoulder, talking, and John lost sight of them in box elder shadow.

He sat up, thrust his feet in jackboots, and stopped. The Pike Country sentry would be prowling around, and an empty bed would encourage suspicion. He lay back, dozing and waking, and next thing he knew it was graying up toward dawn, and Prudence Boomer was banging two skillets together in a breakfast call.

There was more stew and dumplings gulped, and then men hurried away, wiping whiskers with the backs of their hands to pike pole their bullboats back to the Yellowstone's muddy shallows. John worked with the others, and even Shep Shepherd, his arm wrapped in a grimy bandage, did his bit pulling a cordelle. Blackfoot Stillman was gone, but there was nothing strange in that. A scout must range wide of a boat brigade, watching breaks and prairie for danger. The hunter, Rechlin, rode off, driving the horse remuda, his long-barreled H.B.C. fusil held upright, Indian fashion, with bits of colored wool and scalp hair fluttering from its forearm and stock.

The boats were away half an hour before sunrise, riding high, following the crooked channels among mud bars. There was nothing to do for the moment but steer and ride, and a noticeable apprehension settled over the Pike's Peakers.

"Thar she is," John said. "Brulé. Them yellow cutbanks with the coal strips yonder."

They were still four or five miles away. As yet no one mentioned going ashore to scout them for danger. After another mile, Blackfoot Stillman appeared on the prairie rim and rode down across the bottoms, splashing his gotch-eared cayuse through shallow water to the boats.

"Not a damned thing," he ripped out in a voice everyone could hear. "Pounded bush for six or seven mile along Brulé. Maybe some old sign, but hell! . . . the Gros Ventres always camp at Brulé when they cross from the Musselshell." He saw John and nudged his horse closer to the second boat. "What the dirty old hell, John? You been hittin' the snake juice again and seein' things?" He grinned, showing tobacco-browned teeth. An old arrow scar disfigured his left eye, and it made him squint and gave his grin an off-kilter, leering quality.

John laid down his pike pole and tight-roped across the rude catwalk that served to stretch the birch sides of the boat.

The craft was drifting downstream a little, grabbing her bottom against a mud bar, and Blackfoot kept nudging the pony along with his moccasin heels.

"They's Injuns yonder," John said.

"Don't you think I can read sign?"

"You can read 'er. You can smell a moccasin print and tell whether it's Cree, Cheyenne, or Chippeway. That's why I know you're making up your story about Brulé. Maybe you want to git us massacred like you did the factor at Rosebud in 'Fifty-Seven."

Blackfoot heehawed. "What you know about 'Fifty-Seven? You was still robbin' coaches down Californy way in 'Fifty-Seven." He kept laughing in his raucous voice, beating hands against the legs of his dirty buckskin pants. He was careful though not to get his hands near the Texas pistol. Not that he was a coward. He'd fought white, Indian, and half-breed for twenty years. It was just that the quick draw wasn't his game.

He swung his pony around and shouted at the Pike's Peakers. "Tell you what! . . . I'll climb aboard one o' your damn hide boats and ride with you past Brulé yonder. If we collect as many as one arrow or rifle ball, you can shot weight my neck and drown me ten feet deep in Yallerstone mud."

Mast stood on the prow platform of the forward boat. He cupped his hands to shout: "You will like hell! You'll ride the bluffs and make sure. I have a fortune afloat here, and I don't aim on taking a chance."

Blackfoot kept chuckling to himself as his pony churned back through mud to the fetlocks, up the bank, and across the river flats and steep pitches to the prairie edge above. He set his horse long-stirruped like an Indian, his tangled, reddish hair tied in back with red ribbon, bounding in rhythm with the horse. He disappeared, but from time to time one could get a glimpse of him along the edge of prairie.

An hour more, with morning sun growing hot, Brulé was close, its clay bluffs swinging into full view as the boats cleared a willow-grown point. Scarcely a quarter mile off, with the boats still drifting toward it. . . .

Prudence Boomer bellowed: "Pull in, you idiots! I ain't ridin' past that point without lookin' 'er over good."

Jackson, on the steering sweep of the second boat, swung hard, bringing the craft in shore, but Elvis Mast signaled to his steersman, the squat and powerful Dunny Schmidt, to keep going downcurrent.

All except one of the Pike's Peakers were in the second boat. They watched tensely, not saying a word as Mast's bullboat drifted closer and closer to Brulé Point. The current set in there carrying it so close that men had to crouch down and hold their hats on. Nothing happened. A prairie chicken was scared up and flew away, drumming its short wings. If any more proof were needed that no one was lurking at Brulé Point, that prairie chicken was it.

"No ambush!" Boomer grunted, facing his wife with an I-told-you-so.

John said: "And it makes me look like a liar all around. So there's only one thing I can do. Take you ashore and show you Injun sign. It'll be there, and no older'n last night."

There was a campfire, dead and covered with feathery ash. At one side was a hole, large as a small keg, lined with pegged-down buffalo skin, half filled with greasy water and stones. Meat had been boiled there by means of hot stones from the fire. Jackson sniffed the cook hole. Despite the August heat, it had not started to spoil.

"Yesterday."

176

"Sure. And the leaves on those busted willow branches just started to wilt."

They were still examining Indian sign when Mast strode back through the bushes.

"Look old to you?" John asked.

He barely glanced. "Gros Ventres."

John faced the others. "Maybe it is. Maybe not. Maybe it's Blackfoot, or Crow, or North Cheyenne. Anyhow it's Injun, and all of 'em can kill you mighty dead. No squaw sign. No teepee ring. That means a war party. Fifteen or twenty, I'd say by the pony tracks. They must have known I'd sighted 'em and moved on. If they did, it will mean another ambush farther along. Maybe you'll get by this war party. There'll be plenty more trying to lift your hair between here and Fort Union. If you boys want to save your gold, and your scalps to boot, you better leave these bullboats and head for Lone Tree, then on down the Bozeman Trail."

Boomer shook his head. "I ain't runnin' from the first Injun sign."

"That red hair o' yours will look good on a coup stick."

"I ain't runnin'."

The boats went on, working around and over mud bars, and at sundown they found a camping spot at the edge of some wide flats. There the argument was continued. Two factions had evolved with the parson, Prudence Boomer, Red, and Jackson wanting to abandon the river route and go overland, while the others, Mast's men, Cyrus Boomer, and two more Pike's Peakers wanted to stick to the original plan.

"Let 'em take their hide boats to hell if they want," John finally said. "Them as wants can take their stuff to Long Tree."

Red surprised everyone by chiming in: "Sure! Let 'em get killed if they want. I'm for sticking with Comanche John."

Mast had been sitting with his tin plate on his knees. Rage started him lunging across the fire toward the kid. He checked himself. "You see?" he hissed. "He's been talkin' to the kid. I told you all he wanted was to split us up."

Wrangling continued for half an hour, but no one except Red would go so far as to split away from the rest. It was evident that Mast got satisfaction from the way things had ended. He stood, his powerful legs spread wide, muscles molded against the tight-fitting buckskin. He was smiling a little, watching the men leave and start making their beds.

Jennie came up, light-footed as a faun deer, and picked up the bucket. It was the women's nightly job to dip drinking water so it would settle for breakfast. Jennie wore a cotton dress, clean but washed many times, and she was growing out of it. She knew he was looking at her, knew the dress was too small, and her cheeks colored from embarrassment.

"Let me help you, child," Mast said.

He leaned to take the bucket from her. She did not release it. His hand closed on hers. She tried to pull away then, but he held her fast. With casual strength he swung her around and headed her toward the river. Her steps were unwilling, but Mast was not an easy man to resist.

They disappeared in the shadows beyond the upended bullboats. Red had risen to one knee and was crouched forward, staring after them, his reddish complexion turned gray.

"Take it easy, son," John said.

"But damn it all. . . ."

"I said take it easy." He nudged the banjo with his jackboot. "That. Play something."

Red plucked the strings, but his fingers couldn't locate the chords. He was watching the direction where they'd disappeared. He watched for what seemed a long time. Actually it was only a couple or three minutes. No sign of Mast or the

178

girl. It should take no more than half a minute to get the bucket of water. There was no sound save for the gurgle of river, the sounds of men getting inside bedrolls.

Red got to his feet and started down toward the river.

"You stay!" John growled. "I don't think it would be healthful to mix with that rangy-tang."

He tried to shove Red back, but the kid had his jaw thrust out and was stubborn. "Leave me alone. I don't need none o' your help."

John let him go past and slouched after him. His eyes seemed sleepy, but they were taking stock of the camp. French Rechlin was crouched at one side of the fire, a grin on his long-beaked, predatory face. No sign of Shepherd. It always made John suspicious when Shepherd was not in sight. He moved around the buffalo boat. No moon yet. Only starlight. It was a moment before he saw Mast and the girl.

They were near an undercut bank about twenty paces away, bucket fallen at their feet. They were close together, and for a moment he thought Mast was holding the girl in his arms, and that she, with yielding womanliness, had her cheek pressed to his chest. Then he noticed that Mast had twisted her arm behind her, rendering her helpless.

She said something, words coming in a half sob through clenched teeth. She twisted, trying to get away. He was talking to her, quietly, but she wouldn't listen. Red walked toward them with long strides.

"Mast, leave her alone!"

Mast spun, and the girl got away. She backed off, rubbing her wrist, and was ankle-deep in mud before noticing the river. Mast took a step to meet Red, fists knotted and swinging at the ends of his whiplash arms. Red drew up. He stood his ground. One was as tall as the other, but Mast had a massive, muscular thickness in contrast to Red's gangling bones.

"Get going!" Mast hissed, jerking his head toward camp.

"No! I ain't goin' to. You leave her alone. . . ."

"Get going or I'll twist off your rooster neck." Mast started forward, but Jennie flung herself between them. She got hold of Red's arm, trying to drag him away.

"No, Red. You can't fight him. It wasn't anything, Red. He wasn't. . . . Red, take me back to camp."

Red twisted free of her. He thrust her to one side, still facing Mast.

"I ain't scared of you. You leave her alone, d'you hear? All you done since the day you joined up was stare at her and try to get her off alone. And she a poor orphan girl. . . ."

Mast was big, and size made his quickness deceptive. He covered the distance between them with the agility of a mountain cat. His left arm swept Red's guard aside, his right fist smashing him to the ground.

Red struck on his back with such force that his skinny body bounced. He was stunned, arms wide, eyes off focus. After a second he moved, instinctively, dragging himself to a sitting position.

"Mast!" Comanche John barked.

Mast had an uncontrollable temper once it slipped its leash. He started as though to leap on the kid's stomach, stopped, saw Rechlin's saddle gear heaped nearby, snatched an oil-tanned bull-hide quirt from the horn. He swung it high, brought it down with two hundred pounds of power, slashing Red from cheek bone to chin.

He grunted from effort, swung up and down again, again.

John sprang down the bank, grabbed the quirt from behind, drove his knee to Mast's kidney in dragging it free. Attack from that quarter was unexpected. Pain from John's knee momentarily blinded the man, sent him staggering. He almost tripped over Red who sat with both hands clapped over his whip-gashed face.

Mast located John with his savage eyes. He was panting from pain, rage, and exertion.

"I warn you. . . ."

"Past time for warning, Mast. Maybe this is the showdown. Maybe you'd like me to make a carcass o' you right now." John had flung the quirt aside. He stood with arms loose, slouched, eyes narrowed, jaw as always revolving around the chew of tobacco. "Or be you all beller, and no guts for fighting any but gals and slick-jawed kids?"

Mast had got hold of himself. He was frozen-faced, hands on hips, eyes shifting from the twin Navies to John's face. He jerked his head back letting a brittle laugh come through his tight-drawn lips.

"You! Comanche John. The fastest draw artist in the Nor'west. You'd like the excuse to shoot me down."

He was talking too slowly, talking to kill time. The awareness of danger made John's eyes knife around. It was impossible to see through night shadow up the bank. Dirt commenced running in a tiny stream through the washed-out root tangle of the bank. Someone was there. Mast wasn't the type who fought without the percentages weighted in his favor.

John swung his body imperceptibly. The corner of his eye glimpsed gun shine. Atop the bank was Shep with a sawed-off gun.

John turned a little more, apparently slouched and casual. No warning. Only a slight hitch of his shoulder and the right-hand Navy six was out, splitting the night with flame and concussion. There was only the one report and the *thud* of pistol ball striking. There was no outcry, just a man stumbling over

181

boot toes, crashing face foremost through brush and washed-out roots down the bank.

The moon was rising over the horizon. It sent a ray of light across the man's upturned face. It was Shep, all right. There was a round, dark hole in his forehead.

"Thar it be, Shep. What you been a-looking for. Navy slug right betwixt the eyes. I'm a man that believes in keeping his word."

The gun report had started Mast's hand toward the .44, but he checked the movement, backed away, one step, two. John's eyes were never quite off him. Men were shouting, charging down from their beds beneath the bullboats.

Mast spoke: "I told you it would come to this. He killed Shep." He turned and walked toward them. "Did it in cold blood. Shepherd wasn't even armed."

Someone caught sight of Shep's body. The men rushed by. No gun there.

The parson wailed: "What the thunder, John? Why you have to git in these . . . ?"

"Tried to ambush me."

"He ain't got a gun."

"Look atop the bank. He must have dropped it up thar."

Men looked, found nothing. Even with torches from the fire, no gun was found. The half-breed, Rechlin, wandered over, grinning.

"You look for hees sawed-off, *m'shus?* Eet is still in Shep's parflesh bag. Shep, he hasn't carried gun since he's get wounded in arm las' night."

The sawed-off was in the parflesh as Rechlin said.

"That was smooth work, Rechlin," John said, seeming to be good-natured about it all. He spat, wiped black whiskers with the back of his hand. "Yep, smooth work. Bellied up and got it, didn't you?"

Rechlin's lips peeled back in a snarling, coyote expression. "You could make no one believe thees, *m'shu*."

Boomer was already shouting: "It was in cold blood, I tell ye! Shootin' an unarmed man is somethin' I can't stomach. Wounded man to boot."

"Shep was tryin' to ambush him," Red said.

"How do you know?" Mast looked at him contemptuously. "You were there with both hands over your face."

"Yeah, but. . . ."

Jackson broke in: "Were your hands over your face?" Red's expression was admission enough. "Then how'd you know Shep was trying an ambush?"

"He was! Mast carved me with a quirt. John made him quit."

"Then why'd he shoot Shep? It don't make sense."

John started edging away. He'd been in spots like this before. To his mind the most dangerous animal on earth was a Pike County emigrant with a coil of rope. The bank was close, darkness and willows beyond. His horse was yonder. He could cut the picket rope with his Bowie, ride bareback.

"No ye don't, John." It was Prudence Boomer at his back. He stopped, feeling the hard press of the Eight Gauge. He spoke without turning.

"Ye wouldn't do it, Prudence. Not for shooting a bushwhacker. Don't forget the words o' Joshua before the tribes o' Shechem. 'Pity the poor bushwhacker for he shall end his days blasted low by the righteous.' It was a Christian act, Prudence. . . ."

"Ye shot an unarmed man, John. You had it in for him since the first minute."

"He was heeled with that bob-tailed scatter-gun and Rechlin, that snaky 'breed. . . ."

"No use, John."

"I'm goin' over that bank, woman."

"Then you'll do it with your backbone blasted clean through your belly."

She meant it. Too late anyhow. Others were gathering around, two of them with guns unholstered. Sight of the killing had shocked them, made them grim, vengeful. They hadn't liked Shep, but it was hard to remember that, now that he was dead.

Westfall came down from the bullboat plunder box with a coil of rope in his hands.

"I seen it," Westfall said. "I was yonder, just crawled under my blanket. Heard a row goin' on. Shep was atop yonder bank, and John drew and blasted him. Or I guess maybe he had the gun in his hand all the time. Poor Shep just pitched head first, hit the bank, and rolled over like he is now. Never knew what hit him."

Mast's eyes were roving around the circle of grim faces. Satisfaction touched his lips. He said: "You boys decide. I saw it, but leave me out of it. You know what I think of him . . . what I've thought all along. I'd rather see him hanged by your decision."

"Vote it!" rumbled Cyrus Boomer. "I vote for hangin'."

"Hangin'!" said Westfall.

"Hangin'," said Jackson.

"Stretch hees damn' neck lak long fish-eater crane!" cried Rechlin, gesturing with his hands.

The others, one after another, voted for hanging. No one asked Red or the girl. "What say you, Parson?" Boomer demanded.

"I prayed for him," the parson moaned. "I suffered for him, and I saved his ornery hide a dozen times. I ain't askin' you to spare him. All I ask is that you consider the humble start he had, born in a log shanty, brought up on ornery old corn pone and corn likker. Come West and took to bad companions. . . ."

"You vote for hangin', Parson?"

"Every condemned man deserves a few words in his own defense. I'm. . . ."

"You vote yes or no?" Boomer shouted.

"You listen to me!" The parson fastened him with his Old Testament eyes. "John saved all our hides, that worthless one o' yours as well as the rest, if the truth. . . ."

"No use, Parson," John said. "I reckon I had this comin' for quite a spell. Said so yourself. It's fate. Born to git hung. Them's your words. I ain't holding ag'in' none o' you. Reckon we might as well get it over soon as possible. Looks like a good enough cottonwood yonder by the fire."

He walked up the steep pitch from the river, arms lifted, Prudence Boomer's scatter-gun still in his back. He stopped short of the fire.

"Look out for him," Mast said. "He's tricky as a blind rattlesnake."

"Get his guns," said Prudence.

"Hold on." John turned his head to talk to the men behind him. "I got me a last request. I made a promise to the parson that someday I'd unbuckle my gun belts for good and all, and I reckon this is my last chance to make good."

"No!" snarled Mast.

"Little enough to ask," John went on reasonably. "After all, a dying man's last request."

Boomer said: "Go ahead. If he tries anything on that old woman o' mine, we won't be needin' a rope."

"Now, that's for certain." Everyone watched tensely as John's hands dropped slowly to his belts. He unhooked his bullet pouch and powder horn, and tossed them in front of him, unbuckled first one belt, and then the other, letting the heavy Navies swing around and drop to earth a step or so in front of his feet. There was a perceptible easing of tension when it was done and John's hands were once again up in the air.

"Thar they be, Parson," John said mournfully. "Unbuckled for the last time. Sorry it had to be thisaway and not like ye wanted, but I reckon they's some folks that's just bound to get hung."

"Amen, John."

"Amen!" Prudence said it. The scene was getting to be too much for her. She sniffled and wiped her nose, but still kept the old double gun pointed.

John went on in sorrow: "I led me a terrible life. Bad companions right from the start. 'Share and share alike' . . . that was my motto, but it was always with t'other man's gold." He stood with hands clasped, head bowed as though in resignation and prayer, but his eyes, as always, were quick through slitted lids.

The cottonwood had been lightening-shattered and one thick, dead limb big as a man's thigh was thrust over the camp. It seemed to have been created expressly for the grim purpose to which the bullboat men were putting it. Westfall tossed one end of the rope over it, caught it on the downswing, started rolling a hangman's noose. He didn't have the knack of it and, after a couple of unsuccessful tries, turned the job over to Boomer.

John said: "You ain't doing it right. You make a double loop, then bring the free end back with two feet to spare. That makes the knob end that fits beneath a man's ear. All I'm asking is a good knot and a good drop."

Mast ripped out a laugh. "Your kind deserves to strangle slow with your toes one inch off the ground, but I'll see you get a good drop."

He emptied the grub box, set it beneath the limb, placed an upended kettle atop it. By that time Boomer had finished his knot and set the noose to swinging like a slow pendulum alternately in firelight and shadow.

Red's voice suddenly startled them: "Stick up your hands, you dirty stranglers!"

He'd sneaked up from the river, holding a big-bore Jager rifle, and was crouched forward, quirt welts and excitement making his face almost unrecognizable, swinging the rifle back and forth in an attempt to cover them all.

"Drop your guns or I'll pull the trigger. You hear me? The first one that tries anything'll git blasted."

Prudence Boomer swung the double gun over: "I ain't droppin' any gun, Red. And so help me, I'll blow the two legs out from under you with buckshot if you don't put down that old Jager."

"I'll kill you, Prudence, I'll. . . ."

Comanche John said: "Drop the gun, Red. You can't fight 'em all."

"No, I'll. . . ."

Red did not see Jackson coming behind him. Jackson's hand reached around, closed on the Jager with thumb between hammer and percussion cap, making firing impossible.

"Drop it, Kid," he said easily.

Red ripped back and forth, but Jackson was a powerful man, and held him that way, one-handed.

John's Navies lay on the earth a half step away. Even though attention was momentarily distracted, it would have been suicide to have reached for them. There was something else, something he'd done deliberately, apparently without the least significance. He'd started the shedding of his guns by unhooking the powder horn and dropping it. It lay on the ground now, slightly closer than the belts, about two feet in front of his right toe.

John swung around, seeming to watch Red. It was quite natural for him to slide a toe beneath the powder horn. The fire was dying to a broad bed of coals, still intensely hot, flames high as a man's knees.

He casually flipped his toe. The powder horn arched, touched fire, and exploded in a yellow flash of flame and concussion.

The blast struck a blow that drove men backward. It was momentarily deafening and blinding. A gun roared as somebody instinctively pressed a trigger. The bullet went wildly through the night.

Comanche John had plunged forward through flying coals of the fire, snatching his Navies from the ground. He hurdled the blackened area where the fire had been, ran across scattered coals, struck brush, and kept going.

Men had recovered their wits after the momentary shock of explosion. The cursing voice of Elvis Mast rose above the rest, issuing orders, trying to direct pursuit.

John's horse was there, having been driven in with the hunting remuda. He seemed to know. John jerked the picket rope free, coiled it. There was plenty of time now with brush and darkness to cover him. He buckled the Navies back in place, found his saddle, swung on the horse bareback, holding the saddle in front of him, and rode it at an easy pace across the bottoms, up a brush-filled draw to the prairie rim.

There was no pursuit. He saddled, freshened his chew of tobacco, sat with one knee crooked over the horn, watching.

IV

The country looked limitless by moonlight, rolling benches rising step after step, ending in purple mountains, a fine country to be on the loose in. It was a day's ride to Lone Tree. John could get a pack horse there and press on south, past the Big Horns, the Wind Rivers, to the roaring boom camps of Colorado. He should go now, without waiting, and to hell with them. But he didn't. He remained there, slouched forward on the horse, watching.

It was an hour before Blackfoot Stillman rode across the bottoms, and another by the time he'd come back again after his nightly conference with Mast. Blackfoot rode to the prairie, passing within half a mile without noticing Comanche John, and disappeared along a dry wash. After a considerable wait, John followed him.

The man was not scouting. He was riding somewhere, making a beeline, horse alternately at trot and walk. John had to press forward to keep him in sight. Shortly before daylight, Blackfoot disappeared over a coulée rim.

John dismounted, left his pony in a brushy draw, and bellied to the edge. There were a hundred feet of sheer drop, then the bottoms, black with brush and shadow but no movement. The man was already out of sight. After five or six minutes, John mounted and rode a twisting buffalo trail to the bottoms.

Darkness still hung between the steep walls of the coulée, although dawn was brightening the clouds across the sky. He eased along, reached a bend, and caught sight of eighteen or twenty hobbled horses grazing across some grassy flats where the coulée broadened. No teepees. There wouldn't be. This was a war party. These Blackfeet traveled the long sleeps without asking many favors from nature.

He hid his pony among box elders, went on afoot, walking through brush, going belly down through grass and sagebrush. Smoke was rising above the tips of the bluish-leaves of the bullberry bushes. New wood had been heaped on coals not far—about two hundred yards. He lowered himself to a narrow, dirt-sided channel where a stream ran during early summer. It was easy traveling there, and good concealment.

He kept going until the smoke rose close to his right and the sound of voices came to him, voices speaking the Blackfoot tongue. He climbed to the bank and went belly down, inching, parting brush and weeds ahead of him. His eyes caught movement. He raised a trifle. Blackfoot Stillman's horse was there, cropping grass, still saddled and bridled. A camp was just to the right, a little, grassy pocket amid brush.

An Indian was bending over the fire, fanning it with his long, calf-hide breechclout. Flame suddenly broke through, lighting men's faces. It was the same Blackfoot war party he'd seen at Brulé, only now he had a much closer view of them.

Two there he recognized. There was a rangy, savage-faced chief with a puckered tomahawk scar from cheek to collar bone. That was Standing Rattle, a sub chief of the Blackfeet who had been driven off by his own people after murdering old chief Red Crow four years before. The other was a squat half-breed named Gochard. Gochard was dressed in breechclout, leggings, and moccasins, his chest was striped with ocher and vermilion that had become smeared and sweat-streaked from travel. His Indian blood was Gros Ventre. There were a couple of other half-breeds, so this was not a regular war party out to steal horses and lift scalps from the Crows. A war party like this was more brigands, interested in taking a white man's whiskey, guns, and gold dust.

It was a moment before he saw Blackfoot Stillman seated cross-legged beyond the fire. He'd said something to Standing Rattle who was taking his time about answering.

Standing Rattle spoke, using staccato groups of Blackfoot words, emphasizing them with sharp gestures in sign language. He'd waited for three weeks, he said; he was impatient; he wanted to go north, to the Musselshell, and make winter camp, so he would be there, with meat and wood for his teepee, when the hair on his pony grew long.

"Sure, damn ye!" Blackfoot Stillman spat and let his eyes rove around at the others who one after another came and squatted around the fire. There were twenty-one of them. "But I notice every one o' ye has still got his hair. If I hadn't shook ye loose at Brulé, a good half o' ye might be wolf meat right now."

Some of them understood him, and some of them didn't, so he repeated in Blackfoot, using a combination of words and sign language. After he was through, a young Indian, still earning his eagle feathers, loaded three red stone pipes with a mixture of tobacco and red willow bark, lighted them from a blazing twig, and passed them around. They went the circle, each warrior taking three or four puffs from the pipe as it came to him without bothering about the formalities of blowing smoke at earth and sky.

Blackfoot Stillman said: "You do like I say. You bush up at the Little Dry. You savvy 'em, Little Dry? Plenty white man hair."

"Hah!" cried Standing Rattle, contemptuous of scalps. He worked his hands, making signs of gold, whiskey, guns. In response, other Indians stamped moccasins and raised a chattering babble of agreement. "Plenty guns!" said Standing Rattle.

"You're damned right. Plenty gold buys plenty guns."

John lay on his belly, peering through parted twigs of a low-growing buck brush, grinning, thinking about more than half the gold on those bullboats belonging to Mast. It'd be a mean trick to save those Pike's Peakers and let Mast get robbed by this renegade scout of his. He'd give some thought to it on his way back.

It was getting light. Light meant danger. John had learned more than he'd expected to. He moved his hands, braced them to slide his body back, stopped. Stillman's horse had come close and was muzzling the low buck brush right beside him. It suddenly caught man scent and snorted back, jingling his bridle.

The Indians were suddenly silent. John lay without breathing, fingers reaching back, lightly touching the butts of the Navy sixes. The horse stood at a distance with head high, flanks aquiver, and then started cropping grass again.

An Indian said something. John snaked himself, boots first, finding deeper and deeper brush. The dry wash was farther away than he had thought. A couple of Indians were up. One of them walked to where the horse had been, but black dawn shadow prevented him seeing the packed grass where John had been lying.

John lay still until the Indian started prowling along in the other direction, then the dry wash was there, his legs dangling over it. There were pebbles in the streambed's middle, but there was plenty of soft clay to muffle his boots.

A form suddenly loomed on the bank directly above him, the tall Blackfoot who had left the fire to investigate. It was impossible for him to be there, but he was. The dry wash meandered, making a quarter circle around the camp, and he'd simply cut across.

Momentarily both men were jolted to a stop. John could have drawn and killed him, but there was still a chance of not alarming the others.

One of the warrior's moccasins was on the edge level with John's shoulder. After the first instant of surprise, John's hand darted, seized the ankle, and with a powerful snap of his shoulder dragged him over.

The warrior was carrying a long, flintlock rifle. He dropped it going down. He struck his hip at the edge of the bank, twisted over in mid-air, freeing the ankle from John's grasp. His hand came up from the waist of his breechclout, holding a tomahawk. It had a heavy steel head, sharpened keen as a knife. He struck bottom, back against the bank. The tomahawk swung for Comanche John's skull.

John parried it with an upflung forearm. His own right hand swept up, unsheathing the Bowie. The warrior made a grasp for his wrist, but missing the tomahawk blow had carried him off balance. He started to scream, but it ended in a hissing exhalation and the knife blade pinned him to the bank.

John held him a while and let him fall. It had all happened quickly. He wondered if there had been any sound loud enough to arouse the camp. He listened. Voices still came from a distance. He was safe enough.

The Blackfoot was done for, lying on his back, eyes open, staring from a face streaked with war paint, bare to the waist.

A quiver was there, filled with arrows, its seam decorated with bits of scalp, some of it blond-yellow, so he was a great fighter, numbering white men among his victims.

John thrust the man's tomahawk in his own belt, lifted him, carried him a hundred yards, found an undercut bank, caved it over him. They wouldn't search long. War parties like to keep on the move.

It was a long ride back to the river, the cayuse tiring under him. He sighted the bullboats downstream and cut across hilly badlands to reach them. It was late afternoon by then. Today, the Pike's Peakers were in the lead, with Mast's craft a half mile behind.

John waited, keeping out of sight until the current carried the boat in shore, then he rode out with hand uplifted in an Indian sign of peace.

"Blast my hide if it ain't the road agent again!" Prudence bellowed.

"Keep away from that scatter-gun," he called back. "I'm still trying to save your hides."

Jackson drove his pike pole in mud bottom, swinging the boat around so its nose came to a stop in shallow water. He held it there, and like the others watched with silent suspicion while John splashed close on his horse.

The parson said: "You shouldn't have come back here, John. These folks. . . ."

" 'Course I shouldn't have." He stopped, reins looped over the saddle horn, hands free and resting on the legs of his homespuns. "Reckon I could draw and get every damn' one o' ye before you ignorant Pike's Peakers could pull trigger once, so don't get foxy. I'm peaceful. I'm tellin' you what I came to tell, and then you can do what you want and the hell with you." He spattered the side of the bullboat for emphasis.

"Christian duty. You believe in a man doing his Christian duty, don't ye, Prudence?"

She snorted through her nostrils.

He went on: "When that hanging o' yours misfired like a gun loaded with bakin' powder, I rode off, but not far. I had an idee o' following Blackfoot after he came in to report. So I did. He took me straight cross-country to a deep coulée where that renegade war party was making war talk. Bellied up close and risked my hide, but I heard enough to know they planned on making an ambush at the Little Dry. That's yonder about sundown. So thar she is . . . my story. Believe it or not, I ain't giving a particular damn."

Mast's bullboat was swinging close. There were only three in it—Mast, Dunny Schmidt, and Westfall. Both Mast and Schmidt were holding rifles.

"Back again?" Mast hissed the words through set teeth. His eyes roved the others. "Are you still fool enough to listen to him after last night?"

"Maybe we was too hasty last night," Jackson said.

"I suppose he's trying to warn you of another ambush!" Mast let a laugh jerk his shoulders. "One thing about John . . . he can come up with a fresh ambush whenever it's handy."

The parson asked significantly: "How'd you know he was warnin' us of another ambush?"

Mast fastened him with his cold eyes. "I see what you mean. What you're trying to do. You want to make the others suspect that I have some connection with these imaginary Blackfeet." He swung around, face looking big-boned and savage. "Is there anyone here who thinks that?"

"No," Boomer muttered. "Everybody here knows you got more to lose than any of us. You wouldn't be that big a damned fool."

Jackson said: "Well, anyhow, John gave it to us straight

about Brulé Point. Showed us fresh Injun sign there. Now he says we're walkin' into another ambush at the Little Dry."

"How does he know?"

"Followed that renegade scout to their camp. I never did trust him. 'Specially when I heard about that massacre at the Rosebud."

Mast laughed again, this time making it weary and contemptuous. "All right, I give up. I'll not repeat again what this road agent's game is. We went by Brulé without getting a shot fired at us, and we'll go past the Little Dry the same way. I was figuring on a camp spot a couple miles this side of the Dry, but if you're jumpy, let's keep right on drifting and pass it tonight. River's wide there even in low water and we can keep to the south shore out of range. I'll take this boat through first. That satisfy you?"

They were silent for a while, thinking it over. John chewed and spat. "Better come along with me and save your hair."

Jackson shouted: "By damn, I'm a-going to. The hell with this river."

Mast jerked up his rifle, finger crooked on the trigger, but not quite aiming. "We'll stick together, Jackson, just like we voted to. I'll kill the first man who tries to leave the boat."

Jackson lunged toward a rifle leaning against a bale of hides, Boomer stopping him.

"No! He's right. We started out together. We got to see it through together."

The parson said: "Sure we do. We got to stick together."

Comanche John said: "You turn ag'in' me, too, Parson?"

"Voted, didn't we?"

John looked around and recognized the decision. He chewed, spit, and finally asked to come aboard. No one objected, so he cut his pony loose for Rechlin to pick up when he came downriver with the hunting remuda, and climbed over the side.

"Yep. I took cyards in this ignorant game, so there's nothin' I can do now but play my stack out."

V

Thunderclouds came up blue-black, covering the sunset. Here the river cut through broken hills and cutbanks, and at stormy twilight one coulée was deeper, broader than the rest. That was the Little Dry.

John got Red aside and jerked his head at the girl, Jennie. "You keep her behind the bales if there's shooting, d'you understand? If they's any woman kilt, I'd rather it'd be some ornery old galoot like Prudence Boomer."

During the last couple of hours, Mast's boat, carrying a lighter cargo, had moved a considerable distance ahead. With the Little Dry in sight, Mast signaled to Dunny Schmidt who anchored the clumsy craft against a deeply driven pike pole. When the distance had closed down to a hundred yards, Mast signaled for the anchor pole to be withdrawn, and the bullboats went on, carried across wide shallows more by oars and pike poles than the current. Keeping to the south shore, they were well out of rifle range from the Little Dry.

There was no sign of anything. Darkness was settling, thunder—a riffle of wind across the water—some big, warm drops of rain. Darkness was almost complete when Little Dry coulée was at their backs and the quickening current caught them. The storm broke away, opening an area of translucent sky. The moon rose, silvering cloud edges, silhouetting pointed badlands hills. Relief at the passage of apparent danger made everyone on the boat want to talk at once.

Mast, up ahead, was signaling with a lighted candle. He'd found a camp spot, a small flat beyond the first steep bank of the river.

"You see?" His voice was the easiest and most cheerful John could ever recall hearing it. "There was no trouble. But we'd better leave the boats afloat for a while anyhow. It might make some of you feel better."

Everyone had camp duties—anchoring cordelles, carrying supplies, preparing the campsite. Westfall shouldered an axe and started across the flat toward some white-bleached driftwood that high water had carried against the cutbank side of the flat.

He drew up suddenly, and those ashore could hear him say something. He was carrying an old-fashioned single-barrel pistol at his hip. He reached for it, but a *twanging* banjo sound vibrated the air, followed by the *thud* of something striking flesh.

Westfall spun halfway around, sucking breath, head tilted, his distorted features momentarily visible by moonlight. He was clawing at an arrow that had been driven almost through his chest. He went down and out of sight among sagebrush. For a stunned moment no one made a move, then Boomer started across the open moonlight. A gun rocked the air, sending powder flame from among thick-growing bullberries. More shots—gun flame from both ends of the flat—caught the camp in a crossfire.

Boomer was spun around, but not off his feet. He ran back, following the others who scrambled to cover behind the bank.

A Blackfoot war cry pierced the air and riders crashed through brush.

"Come and get it, damn ye!" John roared.

He expected a charge, but it didn't come. Horsemen were shadow shapes crossing the back of the clearing. Gone again. No sound of hoofs. A couple of keelboat men were firing back at the ambushed Indians, blind and unseen.

"Hold it, ye damned fools," Comanche John muttered. "Save your fire. You'll get plenty o' shooting before this night's done with, I'm thinking."

They watched the moon-swept clearing. There was no sign of Indians creeping forward. The shooting continued, slow and methodical, bullets and an occasional arrow. There was no breeze, and the air became strong with powder smoke. A man was cursing through his teeth. Boomer. The bullet had scorched his ribs, and one side of his buckskin shirt was growing heavy from blood.

"John?" It was the parson's voice.

"Here I be."

"How many Injuns out there?"

"I'd guess at four behind each heap o' brush. That means about eleven more that ain't accounted for. Twelve counting Blackfoot Stillman, and thirteen if they fetched Rechlin, which I don't think they did."

"You think Rechlin's in with 'em?"

"Sure. Mast and Dunny Schmidt, too."

"Mast's got more to lose than any of us."

"Parson, I been thinkin' o' that, and I've decided you was a damned old fool."

"I may be an old fool, but I ain't damned."

John chuckled. "Maybe. Keep your eye peeled, Parson. Them others are some place, and there's nobody like a renegade Blackfoot for deviltry."

John moved downstream, keeping to the bank shelter. He came to an undercut point of ground higher than his head and paused there, right-hand Navy drawn, peering through roots that had been washed out by high water.

He saw nothing, heard no sound except for the methodical crash and echo of Indian gunfire. Beyond the point was a stretch of bank, and after that a backwater that ran a hundred yards or so into a high-water channel. Cottonwoods arched on both sides of the backwater, covering it with darkness.

A moment before the backwater had been flat as a mirror. Now, although there was no breath of wind, little choppy waves distorted the slight reflections. Something was moving through shallow water.

John backed away, motioned to the parson, Jackson, the Boomers. No sign of Mast or Dunny Schmidt, but for the moment he had no time to investigate.

"What is it?" Boomer muttered.

John jerked his head, indicating the disturbed water. No one appeared to see anything strange about it.

"Waves. They figure on getting us along the bank, or from behind that downriver bullboat."

Boomer had a big-bore rifle and a dragoon pistol that was a two-hand job to lift, Prudence had her double gun, Jackson a Navy and his Jager rifle, and even the parson had rounded up an old, long-barreled fusil. John groaned. They'd raise hell for a few seconds anyway.

Red came up, and John hissed at him: "Dammit, I said for you to stick by the gal."

"She's here, too. I can't. . . ."

"Ever try to reason with a woman?" Boomer muttered.

"If I had that Prudence o' your'n," John said, "I'd have her taller-shining my jackboots in a week."

Prudence said: "Inside a week I'd have you washed, shaved, and laid out for buryin'."

The water disturbance was worse now. Little, rolling waves bounded *slap-slapping* to the bank almost at their feet. From the darkness came the sucking sound of a foot being withdrawn from mud.

A form became visible. It was a man, climbing across driftwood that divided the backwater from the narrow strip of shore, still thirty or forty yards away. Boomer twitched, started forward, rifle up.

John hissed: "Damn ye! If you blast that buffalo gun, I'll split your skull with my tomahawk."

Boomer eased back, exhaling, getting his finger off the trigger. Excitement made him wheeze through his nostrils. No harm in that. Gun echo, the occasional shout of an Indian, covered it.

Other forms, one after another, crossed the point and became lost again in bank shadow. John counted them. Fourteen.

They were coming slowly, creeping in utter silence. The river was on one side, the steep bank at the other. Moonlight struck them, bringing to life the white and yellow paint streaks across chests, arms, faces. John wriggled back a trifle, glanced to see the waiting guns.

"Ready?"

"I'm ready," Prudence muttered.

John spat, chose two of the more distant forms, hesitated a brief instant to aim, and the two Navies ripped the night, one close on the other. A high, wavering scream started from an Indian's throat, but it was drowned by the concerted roar of concussion flame and ripping lead that John's shots had touched off.

Indians fired wildly, splashed through water. One started

climbing the bank, was hit, fell back with arms flung spread-eagle.

Others might have dashed in flight, too, but Standing Rattle's voice barked orders, stopping them. From the mêlée left by the first volley came Standing Rattle himself, charging forward, tomahawk in one hand, pistol in the other. Others followed, trampling the fallen. Gunsmoke hung thick, and they were distorted shadow shapes, charging through it.

Boomer was fired dry. He lunged to his feet, feeling for a long-bladed skinning knife at his waist.

"Git out o' my way!" bellowed Prudence.

She still had not pulled trigger on the double-gun. She waited until the rush of Blackfeet was almost upon them, then the gun bucked and soared, hurtling shot into the thick of charging bodies.

"Ya-hoo!" shouted John. "Give 'em their belly's full of that squaw gun, Prudence."

Standing Rattle was still in the lead. The second charge of buckshot struck him waist high. The shocking power of the old Eight Gauge smashed him half around and left him broken and lifeless at the bottom of the bank.

Others charged over him, overrunning the point. John fired the last two charges in his Navies, thrust them back, and his hands came up with Bowie and tomahawk.

"Git your bellys full, ye red renegades! This yere is Comanche John, the one they write music about!"

A warrior swung at him and rushed on to attack Boomer. A second one was there, double-barreled horse pistol in one hand, lance in the other.

The warrior pulled trigger as John's tomahawk swung, striking his arm. The bullet was deflected, powder scorching the side of John's face, leaving him half blinded.

The Indian lifted his war lance high, ready to plunge its

heavy H.B.C. trade head through John's breast. Prudence Boomer smashed him to earth with the butt of her Eight Gauge.

"Tha's somethin' to think over next time you tackle Christian folk!" she bellowed.

The charge was broken. Three were down nearby, and more at the bank's edge. Renegades crawled away through the brush. It was hard to tell much through the darkness and powder smoke.

"After 'em!" Prudence said. She was ramming shot and wad down her double gun. "Don't let 'em re-form."

"What's wrong, Jackson?" It was the parson.

"Never mind me. I got to tie this leg up before I bleed to death. Load this Navy and git over the bank with Prudence. There's nothin' like a good slug o' lead in the rump to keep 'em goin'."

Prudence and the parson met with one lonely shot atop the bank, and a blast of buckshot put that single renegade to flight. John was on one knee, feeling for his powder horn. He cursed, recalling that he had none.

He remembered Mast. There had been no sign of him during the charge, no gunfire from up the bank where he and Dunny Schmidt had been posted. He looked around, noticed the Pike's Peakers' bullboat cut loose and drifting slowly, swinging through dead water, feeling for the current.

Red had loaded the Jager and was ramming a charge down the throat of an old-fashioned horse pistol.

"I'll take it," John muttered, shedding his Navies in its place. He plunged knee-deep with mud sucking at his jackboots.

The water was deeper than he thought. He lunged forward, half fell, seized the bullboat's edge, and dragged himself over.

A heavy man loomed above. Dunny Schmidt. He jerked the pike pole he was using and tried to club it aside John's head. He was too close. John rose, fending it off, and smashed the squat keelboat man down with a blow of the horse pistol.

Dunny Schmidt went backward on rubber legs and spilled over the side and lay threshing, half conscious, in muck and shallow water.

"What the hell, Dunny?" A voice came from up front, a man hidden by cargo. It was Blackfoot Stillman's voice. The renegade scout was there with Mast. He must have sneaked over during the Indian charge. "Dunny?" he repeated, coming forward, balancing himself on the rude *passe en avant*.

He recognized John and tried to lunge back. A pistol was in his hand. His foot slipped, and he fell, striking his arm across the spring-pole *passe en avant*. The jar seemed to explode the pistol. A bullet tore up wet splinters. The shot load Red had packed into the horse pistol smashed him to the bottom.

Mast had been at the forward end, working a sweep. He hadn't realized anything was wrong until the twin explosions roared. He dropped the sweep, went for his .44, but John dived over cargo, tomahawk in his hand.

Mast met him, his gun half drawn. He let it fall, side-stepped over tricky footing, seized John's wrist, and forced the tomahawk aside.

They staggered across the boat's pole bottom. John instantly realized that there was no chance for him in a simple contest of strength. He let the tomahawk fall, bending double at the same instant. The weapon was on the flooring poles. He intended to snatch it up with the other hand, swing its sharp blade in an upward motion. But Mast had survived in a half hundred bloody battles along the fur frontier and knew every knife and tomahawk trick. He twisted back, booted the tomahawk away so it disappeared in the two or three inches of bilge water that had seeped through the water-logged buffalo hides.

He came up with right and left hand blows, fists like sledges, bludgeoning John's head from side to side. His knee came up aimed for the groin. John managed to turn enough to take it on the hip bone. He was groggy. The slick pole flooring was under his hands. That was his first realization of being down.

Mast was over him, a Green River knife drawn. He swung it high and drove it for the kidney in a death blow.

John hurtled forward, driving back and aside to Mast's knees. The impact carried the big man off balance and the knife missed, its blade stabbing a bale of buffalo hides. The hides were damp from careless handling. They held the point for an instant. Mast jerked twice before freeing it.

It gave John a few seconds. He rolled over, came up with his own Bowie. Mast's left hand was thrust out, and John reached in an identical movement. He stopped, whiskers parted in a grin.

"Horse and alligator style?"

It was the traditional duel of the keelboat men, fighting it out "half horse, half alligator". Left hands locked together, knives in the right—they would go anywhere the battle took them, land, boat, muck, or water.

Mast stood, arm extended, knife held underhand. It seemed to take him a second to comprehend. Then his lips peeled back, showing teeth in a savage grin.

"Sure. Horse and alligator."

Their hands met, fingers twined. For a moment it was a straight-armed contest of strength with John being forced to retreat. John gave slowly, exhaling deeply, building up his bodily supply of oxygen. He watched Mast's eyes for warning.

Suddenly Mast's arm bent. He tried to snap John forward against the lashing blade of his Green River knife.

It was the simplest trick of such a fight, and John was set for it. He did not battle the strength of Mast's arm. He'd have been killed doing that. Instead, he hurled himself wide, feet off the bottom of the boat, clearing the gunwale. The Green River knife barely nicked his flying buckskin shirt.

At the final instant, Mast tried to shake free. There was no chance of that, no breaking that locked grip. John's weight drew him head foremost and they struck water, spread at arm's length—sank.

The current caught them and twisted them over. There was no sense of direction in the river's pressing blackness. John lashed with the Bowie; an instant later he felt the sting of the Green River knife across his shoulder. Everything was different underwater. Even the burn of a blade striking flesh was deadened.

The mud bottom was thick and clinging. It grabbed a man, slowing every movement, making him feel like a fly must feel when caught in molasses. It grabbed John's jackboots and he made no attempt to fight against it. He utilized it, an anchor, doubling his left arm as Mast had done in the boat above, swinging the Bowie in a horizontal arc.

It struck. No telling where. Not a deadly blow. Not deep enough. The blade was free. He knew the responding stroke would come, straightened his arm trying to parry it. Mast swung around atop him. His knee was bearing down, pinning John's knife arm in the mud. John let his left hand relax—jerked it free. He sensed the knife coming, caught the blow with his forearm. His hand moved up, found Mast's wrist, and with a roll of his body drove the Green

River knife deeply in mud.

He rolled on, pinning Mast's arm under him. Mast let go and lashed like a snared fish trying to free himself. John did not struggle with him. He lay stiff, clenching his teeth, saving his reserve of oxygen. He held until his lungs seemed ready to burst and white lights danced across his eyes.

Mast's struggles became weak and futile. He hadn't taken the deep breaths John had, hadn't even the time to fill his lungs before plunging overboard.

John rolled, crawled through mud. He wasn't holding Mast now. There was no need. He found the edge of Mast's buckskin shirt, plunged the Bowie through it, pinning him to the mud bottom. Then he fought to an upright position, stood. He was in water to his armpits.

He coughed up mouthfuls of river, filled his lungs. There was no sign of Mast. He worked his boots, slowly freeing them, and waded toward shore. Shooting was sporadic a couple hundred yards away, most of it against the cutbank side of the clearing.

From the shore he turned again to watch the river. It flowed placidly beneath the moonlight. Mast was still pinned down out there, but now only the devil himself knew where.

Comanche John followed the shore downstream until he found the keelboat in which Mast had tried to escape. He waded to the mud bar on which it was hung up, went aboard, and was hefting bags of gold dust when the Pike's Peakers came up.

"Hold your fire," he said. "I ain't taking any color. Whar's Mast's gold?"

"In the other boat."

"Let's look at 'er."

"What's he talkin' about?" Prudence bellowed. "The gold belongs to Mast. We can't. . . ."

"I don't reckon he'll object."

They went back, and John opened one of the buckskin bags. He grunted and flung it on the bank, strewing half its contents.

"That's his gold! Birdshot with a few bucks for nuggets. He didn't own any color. Never was a miner. He was a renegade fur trader. That's how he knew Standing Rattle and could make a deal with him to raid this outfit. Standing Rattle wanted guns, and Mast wanted the gold."

He went ashore. There was a knife wound in his shoulder, but the state of his buckskin shirt seemed to worry him more. His boots were starting to dry, and he kept moving to keep them from getting stiff.

Red was loading powder and ball into the Navy Colts while Jennie leaned over, handing him the things he needed.

"Parson," John said, looking at the young couple, "reckon we'll have a weddin' before we fetch Fort Union, or Lone Tree, or wherever we're headed."

He took the Navies, examined the priming, and restrapped them around his drying homespuns. Boomer was lying on a blanket, complaining while Prudence bandaged his bullet-scorched ribs.

John said: "By dang, if that Blackfoot bullet had only come three inches farther south, Prudence and I could have made it a double wedding." He thought it over, and, as he thought, his eyes narrowed and his hands closed on the Navy butts. " 'Tain't too late. I got me a notion to make a widda of you right now."

"Go 'way!" roared Prudence. "Go 'way, ye tabacca-spittin', black-whiskered woolly wolf. Iffen I get rid o' this man varmint I got, do you think I'd ever be danged idiot enough to get hitched with another one?"

THE ADVENTURES OF COMANCHE JOHN

DAN CUSHMAN

Comanche John is a notorious road agent. If he has a last name, no one knows it. Yet his legend precedes him in the form of frontier ballads sung by teamsters and stagecoach drivers. His life is filled with danger and conflict, and although his activities often place him on the wrong side of the law, more often than not he ends up defending the innocent and fighting for what's right. *The Adventures of Comanche John* brings the reader into the thrilling world of Montana mining camps, wagon trains on the Oregon Trail, and stagecoaches everywhere.